Darkness Comes This Way

Book One: Guardians of the Night

Pixie Lynn Whitfield

Stewart

"No notice is taken of a little evil, but when it increases it strikes the eye."

—Aristotle

One

Rogues.

Disgusting vile creatures that Zarah is out to destroy.

The ironic thing is...she used to be one of them.

"See you tomorrow!" the young girl called out as she left the restaurant. Her feet ached from her long shift and she couldn't wait to get home to soak them. It was late and eerily silent while she walked the four blocks toward her apartment building. The moon was hidden through the growing storm clouds, and street lamps were few and far between along the jagged narrow walkways of the empty streets.

The Guardian was hidden in the shadows,

watching the human, knowing from a deep sense that trouble approached and began to follow at a distance between the shadows of the looming buildings. The smell of monster was in the air. The girl was walking to her death. Leaping onto the nearest roof, the Guardian had a mission to do.

The waitress hadn't made it a full block when noises began to sound in her ears. Deep, dark laughter suddenly surrounded her, making her heart race and her steps pick up speed. The clacking of her heels echoed off the concrete sidewalk. Her eyes darted every which way and her blonde-bobbed hair twirled around her face, but she couldn't find the source of the noise. It had disappeared, seemingly to suck her breath away with it. When she took in a shaking lungful of air, she felt her entire body tremble.

"Just the wind," she tried to assure herself out loud, knowing well enough that she was lying. There wasn't any wind, and if there were, it certainly wouldn't have sounded like that.

A low whistle sounded beside her, making her jump. She dropped her purse and the contents of it spilled out onto the walkway. Fear had consumed her enough by then that she couldn't release the scream bubbling at the base of her throat. She turned around to see a tall man leaning casually against a building wall. His head hung down and long, dark hair covered his face. A heavy leather duster jacket wrapped around him, but it did not hide his bulky, muscular frame. She was passing him, trying to avoid staring, when he finally spoke.

"It's a dark night for such a beautiful being like yourself to be walking alone."

The husky edge to his voice made her blood turn to ice. She froze when he stepped out, blocking the path. Fearfully, she scanned the area, hoping to see someone who could help. Something wasn't right about this strange man. Something screamed *danger* to her.

She didn't see the Guardian rushing to get

there before it was too late.

She glanced nervously up at him to see that he had raised his head to look at her, and it was cocked to the side as if he were a curious cat.

It was then that she saw his eyes—a bright scarlet red that showed a threatening hunger. He offered her a wicked smile, and in turn revealed a set of long, white fangs. Her eyes widened in horror and instinct kicked in, causing her legs to finally move as she tried to run from whatever he was. He was a monster from her nightmares—fairytales she was told as a child—but she wasn't dreaming now. He was fast, and quickly snatched her by the waist before she could manage to take two full steps. His hands were large and held her in place. She was unable to get away from his bruising grasp no matter how much she struggled.

She screamed and kicked with wild fever, trying to fight the strange man's grip, but to no avail as he raised her inches above the pavement and began to carry her backward. He pulled her toward the alley with his hand clamped hard over her mouth to silence her. Within seconds they both disappeared into the dark depths of the alleyway, leaving her spilled purse behind under the dim orange street lamp.

The creature's heightened senses became more acute while he feasted, like that of a lion enjoying its prey but remaining aware of its surroundings. The human had been particularly tasteful, satisfying his never-ending thirst. Her life force flowed through him and he could feel his addiction being briefly fed.

His focus on the kill had distracted him because he was soon faced with a gun to his temple. The cold metal against his own dead skin gave him chills. He was weaponless and he could smell the silver bullets inside the chamber of the pistol. The click of the weapon's safety switching off echoed around the stone walls of the surrounding buildings and it made him shudder involuntarily.

He took a deep breath, allowing the scents of the night to wrap around him and wind their way up through his nostrils. Blood from his meal mixed with the light drizzle that had started. And then he smelled the presence of the being that stood beside him. It was one of them: a Guardian.

And it was the rarest one of them all: It was *her*.

Her unique scent of pineapples and lilies filled the air around him. A low, satisfied growl came from deep within his chest. As he stared at the brick wall in front of him with the gun still at his head, his lips curled into a smirk. He may be about to die, but she was in for something interesting in the near future herself. He didn't have to look back at her. He wasn't going to be like the others and try to fight. It would be no use against this Guardian. She was ruthless, and always had been. But at least he could leave her with some last surprises.

The human was already dead, still in his arms, and the creature knew he was about to join her. At least he had enjoyed a good last meal, he mused, staring down at the young waitress' lifeless wide-brown eyes. Her mouth was set in a permanent silent scream.

"You're next," he rasped, speaking to his executioner behind him.

Without a word, the Guardian fired.

*****

Zarah Duncan stared down at the dead Rogue with disgust. The silver bullet was lodged in the side of his head. His body would remain there until morning, when the rising sun would turn it to ash and dust. Passing humans would just think it was a pile of street filth. If only they knew how close to the truth they were...

"Zarah?" A voice sounded through the earpiece she wore.

"Present." The voice chuckled lightly back

into her ear at her sarcastic reply.

"It's time to get back to the Compound. The sun will be up soon." She was ordered by the other line.

"Right away, boss. I just need to take care of a little business first." She stared down at the corpse of the human girl. The creature would be taken care of by the sunlight, destroying that part of the evidence, but the human would not be. Zarah needed to get the body to an area where it would be easily discovered and taken to a proper place. The bite marks on the girl's neck were barely visible, but the humans had advanced drastically over the years with science and technology in medicine. Zarah didn't understand most of it, only they had some insane fancy machines that seemed to do some crazy readings and scans and their doctors were exceptionally more skilled during the autopsies than fifty years ago.

Silently, she knelt down and licked her fingers before placing them over the wounds.

Within seconds, the saliva healed the marks, erasing the traces of what had happened. If it was one thing Vampires were good at, it was covering tracks to keep their existence a secret.

"I called and told you to get back here a little over an hour ago!" Zarah's boss fumed when she entered the Compound, throwing her gun holster down on the nearest table and slipping out of her boots.

She looked up at him angrily and hissed, her fangs revealed in the fluorescent lights.

"I was taking care of a clean-up." She argued. She knew he had only been worried that one of his best residents had nearly been caught out in the deadly light, but she wasn't in a particularly good mood at the moment. Everyone in the Compound knew not to cross her after a night out hunting until after she got her sleep. Not to add to the fact that she had lost the victim. The poor girl was probably no older than eighteen and working that job to pay for college.

"I'm sorry, Zarah. I was just worried about you, as I always am," he replied softly, confirming her initial thoughts. She looked up at him and nodded as she continued to shed more hidden weaponry onto the table. She took a deep breath and calmed her temper; she knew she'd never be able to remain too angry at him for long. Her boss, Nathanial Bolt, had been more like a father figure to her through the years. Life had not been kind to her, but he had been.

In fact, he was the one who had saved her during that time...

"I have some news to share before you take your slumber. Please follow me to the meeting room," Nathanial instructed, interrupting her thoughts. He always knew when she was drifting into that ugly past—and would keep her from doing so by distracting her with conversation. Unfortunately, he could only do that when he was around. When she was alone, she was left with thoughts and memories as she fought the growing insanity within her.

Silently and slowly, she followed him down the long, twisting corridors of the underground building. Her home. She watched him moving in front of her, hoping there would be an explanation along the way, but he remained quiet with his eyes ahead and a blank expression on his face. He was tall, towering above her small frame, and very slender. If one looked at him, they would think he was sickly and weak—but Zarah knew better. Nathanial held a grace about him that almost spoke of royalty. His hair was long, and a brilliant white so bright that it seemed to glow beneath the lights. His skin was just as pale, matching perfectly.

He led her through a set of double glass doors, into a room with a long black wooden table and large leather chairs. It was their meeting room, but rarely used.

"What is he doing here?" she snapped furiously when she eyed one of the Compound residents sitting in one of the chairs at the far end of the room.

"I've asked Draven to be here, Zarah. Calm down." Nathanial motioned for her to take a seat. He sounded aggravated already and let out a frustrated sigh.

She sat as far as she could from the Guardian that was in the room, glancing over at him with a look of hatred. He looked at her, his periwinkle eyes dancing with humor. His dark hair was thick and shaggy, just resting slightly above his shoulders, and despite how handsome he was, Draven Kinsley had given her a hard time since she had returned. She wasn't fond of him in the least. She assumed the feeling was mutual.

He was leaning back in the leather swivel chair, with his feet rested up on the table and his arms placed behind his head, looking well-relaxed. She furrowed her eyebrows in annoyance.

"Can we hurry this? I'm tired." Zarah turned

to Nathanial, looking bored.

"I know, so I'm going to make this short, sweet, and to the point." Nathanial remained standing, his hands on the table, leaning over and glancing between the two of them as he spoke.

"I've called you both in here because there's been an increase in activity as I'm sure you've noticed. I'm pairing Guardians up from now on—and the two of you will be working together."

"You're pairing me up with a Rogue?!" Draven jumped up, shouting furiously, his light Irish accent more noticeable through his anger. Zarah stood as well and growled in warning at him.

"I'm clean," she hissed through her teeth. He shrugged as if he didn't care what she said and rolled his eyes.

Nathanial took his time, and watched the scene play out with interest before he interrupted.

"I'm pairing you up because you're both the best I have. That's final." There was authority in his voice that wasn't there before. Zarah's eyes narrowed, first at Nathanial, then at Draven.

"This is a bad idea," she argued.

"Yeah, she'll probably turn me rabid," Draven said with a snort. Every ounce of control that Zarah had tried to contain, snapped. With intense speed, and before Nathanial could comprehend what was happening, she ran at Draven and shoved him into the wall. He tried to block her punch, but her anger outweighed his instinct and he was too slow.

"Crazy bitch!" Draven screamed in rage after Nathanial pulled Zarah off of him.

She flipped him off in response.

"Enough!" Nathanial shouted so loud that it caused the glass room to vibrate. Passing Guardians and workers stopped to stare.

"You two will have to learn to get along!" he bellowed again, still gripping Zarah by the shoulder. No matter how frail her boss looked at times, she could feel his strength in the grasp he had on her. Draven stood. The cut on his lip already began to heal.

"I'm putting my full trust in you both to behave and try to get along enough to get the jobs done. You're like children to me and I will not tolerate this rivalry." Nathanial lowered his voice, releasing Zarah. He was wary, and continued watching her, remaining close to her side in case he needed to break apart another fight.

Draven glared at her silently for a few long seconds before he finally nodded in an unspoken agreement to make an effort to work with her.

Satisfied, Nathanial left the meeting room muttering under his breath.

"No turning guns on me," Draven warned on his way out, starting to pass by her. His eyes watched her hands in precaution.

"Trust me, if I had wanted to kill you just then, I would have," she said in a mocking tone, pulling a small pistol from behind her back. He stared at her in shock, frozen in place and didn't say another word.

She smirked as she walked past him out of the room, heading toward her own for bed.

"Be ready at eight, Draven," she called over her shoulder before she disappeared behind a corner.

Two

In a world where good and evil mingled, there laid another beneath it. An underground of night creatures—Vampires—of which the humans were completely oblivious to.

The humans that did come close to discovering the truth either quickly forgot from a magically induced hypnosis, or died at the hands of a blood thirsty monster.

The Vampires were divided. Rogues were often loners, rarely found living among any other rabid, and as far from socialization with each other as they could get when possible. They hid out during the daylight hours in abandoned warehouses or burrowed into the ground at old cemeteries.

There were others, too, who weren't rabid or

the fierce protecting fighters that Zarah worked with. These were the Hiders and they lived in large groups mostly, in homes, and went about life normally—sometimes pretending to be human and asked to be left alone by the Guardians. They got their blood through blood banks or volunteer donors. This was the same mannerisms in how the Guardians fed as well. Although live human feedings were rare at the Compound. This was something done only in emergency cases.

The Guardians were established over a hundred and fifty years ago to fight against the rabids. With their growing numbers through the years, more Guardians came in and trained to be on the elite team of warriors.

And then there was Zarah. Different. Unique. Unlike any of them. She was the outcast in a world full of strange creatures.

Once a vampire turned Rogue, there was no going back to the way things were. Their addiction to the blood was like a crack-addicted human to the tenth degree. It was never-ending, causing the creature to follow a life of killing for more to try and satiate their immense thirst. The being lost all intelligence and control.

Until a Guardian would seek them out to destroy.

But something was unusual about Zarah. She had been Rogue for almost a full year until Nathanial brought her to the Compound.

Zarah went back while others hadn't. She'd survived, cured from the rabid state of mind...

And she didn't know why...

Blood was everywhere. Splashed upon the walls, a dark scarlet stained the white carpet as the color of her destruction stood out around her. At her feet, lay three bodies. Her eyes were wild with a raging hunger she couldn't contain...and a small, dark voice was laughing maniacally through her thoughts.

Somewhere nearby, she could faintly pick up the scent of jasmine and lily, despite the strong metallic odor that already filled her nostrils from the deaths she caused. Her eyes darted across the room to see a vase. White flowers stood out—the source of the soft floral scents that she had picked up on. But even they were stained with spots of the crimson liquid that she'd just murdered for...

And then she wept, her screams of anguish breaking the silence of the night as she collapsed on the floor to cry out her tortured mind.

Zarah awoke with an abrupt start, sitting straight up in her bed to gasp for air. The memories always haunted her, even in her dreams. Still, each time they left her feeling tormented and horrific.

It took her awhile to calm her breathing and to realize she wasn't in that place of mind anymore. She was a Guardian again. No longer a Rogue.

She'd never be able to shake the images of things she had done though.

Looking around as she calmed herself, she was thankful to be back at the Compound in her living quarters. It was a small apartment with an open bedroom, sitting area and kitchen all in one space, and a simple bathroom with a shower stall. Nothing entirely fancy, but suitable for her nonetheless.

The buzz of the alarm on her bedside table screeched annoyingly loud when it went off seconds later and she reached over to hit it. In recent months, she was always awake before the blasting thing sounded off. She didn't know why she bothered setting it anymore.

"Damn it, there goes another one," she muttered out loud as she hit the device a little too hard, causing it to break. Its beeping died slowly, sounding fast and high-pitched at first before it became low and soft. It was the fourth one she'd broke in the last month.

Grabbing it, she stood and tossed the little round brass clock in the silver trashcan near her bed before continuing on to the kitchen for a drink.

Her quarters became flooded with a bright, white fluorescent light when she flipped the switch. She didn't need much in this place because of her limited diet, but she did have a refrigerator stocked with her one need: blood. Blood that their kind tended to con out of the humans by setting up fake blood banks and traveling buses, or stealing from the local hospital. Sure, they were deceiving the humans most times, but it was better than them running out to feed on people. They preferred to stay a secretive race. It prevented panics and wars.

She had hers in fancy, dark bottles. In the same way that some people rather have their alcoholic beverages in bottles instead of cans, she'd rather have her drink in a bottle instead of a plastic bag.

As she drank standing at the white kitchen counter, she scanned her living area. It was small, but she was content there at the Compound. The kitchen was tiled with a black and white checked pattern. The bedroom area, which opened out from her kitchen, was carpeted with a plush crème color. Her bed was pushed against the wall on the other side of the room; across from that was a small television on a black iron stand. She hardly watched the thing, but it had been provided by Nathanial when she was in recovery a year prior. There was a closet near the bed where she kept her weapons and clothes, just enough space for those things and not much else. On the wall above her was a large rectangular mirror with a black iron frame to match the television stand. Beside the bed were stacks of books and craft supplies—showing some semblance of life and personality outside of fighting. They weren't very organized, scattered every which way throughout the corner, but still unusually neat in its own way as if she had a particular order of things.

    Her gaze lingered momentarily on the mirror as she watched herself drink from her cloudy amber-colored bottle of scarlet deliciousness. The flavors danced wildly over her tongue and brought back many different memories. Most of which she wanted no part in.

Zarah almost snorted out loud to herself as she looked over her reflection. Humans had the crazy notion that vampires couldn't see their own reflections. She always found that funny in an odd way, although she didn't know why. They also had made many misconceptions of the vampire legend in general.

Wooden stakes, garlic, holy water? She laughed at it all and always shook her head when she'd pass by some young naïve humans discussing the 'legend' or would read the latest stupid human romantic novel about vampires and humans. *'Let them believe what they want. It's the best thing for them, rather than being forced into the reality of our world,'* she had always thought to herself.

The fan kicked on, sending frosty air through

the vents above her head and her hair flew lightly in the fake breeze. She glanced at the mirror again as she finished her bottle and looked herself over with curiosity. Her long, dark auburn hair swayed slightly around her face, which still held the innocence of the day she had been turned four decades before. She had barely just turned nineteen years old then.

Her long exotic lashes were a deep ebony and stood out against her pale skin. Her amethyst and turquoise colored eyes were a unique trait—the two colors combined in a swirl in her irises.

She wasn't tall, only standing around five foot and three inches in height. Her body was lean and beautifully curved, yet athletic and prepared for a fight.

She never could quite understand her appearance. She felt different compared to the other Guardians. Most were tall and more built than her. Most were also men; she was one of the rare women on the team.

Zarah glanced up at the white clock on the kitchen wall and sighed. She needed to get dressed to go meet Draven for a night out hunting. She was not the least bit thrilled about this idea. Being paired up with anyone else wouldn't have made much of a difference. They all feared her, ignored her, hated her. She was the Compound Freak. Draven was just the most open about it. Nathanial, however, must have had a legitimate reason in pairing up the Guardians. Maybe there was something he knew that he hadn't informed anyone of yet.

She had certainly noticed something odd the night before in her encounter with that Rogue. She couldn't bring herself to tell anyone about it at the time. He spoke to her, gave her some kind of warning as if he knew her. Something was going to happen. It was all strange. She ignored it for the moment until she could get more information. Maybe she'd just been tired and had been imagining the words?

Zarah didn't dress like the other Compound Guardians either. While they normally donned themselves in fancy military-like black gear, she dressed entirely different. That night she wore a pair of ripped, faded blue jeans and a cotton purple tank top with a long, black duster jacket that reached down to her calves. If it weren't for the gun holster that she needed to wrap around her back and onto her shoulders, she probably wouldn't even wear the jacket. She did love her boots though. They were old worn black combat-style boots that laced up to the tops of her ankles. The leather had wrinkles in it from intense wear and action, but they were comfortable. Comfort was important when chasing after those nasty things.

Once ready, she walked out into the hallway, locking her door behind her with a swipe of her electronic card key. The clean white tile and shiny glossed walls gleamed from the bright lights. The Compound almost had the appearance of a hospital wing, white and sterile, with chrome framed light fixtures lining the top of the walls near the ceiling.

She made her way around the winding corners, walking with confidence, as she searched for her new partner. There were only two places that he'd probably be at that time of evening—the Lounge, or in his room.

She knocked on his door, but when he didn't answer, she headed toward the other area where she knew she could find him.

The Lounge was a large room in the Compound where Guardians would go to be social with others, enjoy drinks, read, watch television, and do whatever else. It was, in a sense, a common area. From time to time, parties were held there. Zarah never attended. She was never invited.

"Ready?" she asked emotionless when she found him sitting in one of the large black leather chairs reading a paper.

Draven looked up at her and shrugged nonchalantly. He hated the partnering idea as much as she did.

She stared down at him with impatience, noting that he also didn't seem to dress in the usual military-style garb. Instead, he wore baggy, rugged black jeans, a plain white tee shirt and a black trench coat. His hair was pulled neatly back in a low ponytail.

He stood, and she realized for the first time how incredibly tall he was compared to her small stature. It was a bit intimidating.

"Yeah, let's go and get this over with." He sounded agitated. She frowned and reached out to grab his arm.

"I don't like this arrangement either, but we can at least try to work together professionally for the sake of Nathanial," she said through clenched teeth. He yanked his arm away from her out of anger and turned his mouth up in disgust. She recoiled at the sight of his fangs.

"I know. Here's the deal—no personal talk. Work only," he growled.

She nodded and rolled her eyes, pretending to ignore the inkling of fear that had momentarily struck her.

"Like I would want to talk to you in that way," she mumbled as they began to head out of the Lounge.

They remained silent from then until they exited the elevator to the garage.

The Compound was underground, hidden from human view. Once outside, they were immediately in a parking garage outside of a sky rise apartment building. When the humans were in the elevator, they didn't notice a small black button that was shielded behind a metal plate. So to them, the only direction the lower level elevator could go was up. It had its down button, but it would only work from the upper floors and bring them down to level one of the garage. To go down to the Compound, a Guardian would use a special key to slide the metal plate away and push the black button.

"Your car or mine?" Draven asked when they entered the garage. The air was chilly and the smell of wet concrete from rain earlier filled their senses.

"I don't have a car. I normally walk."

He sighed and motioned for her to follow him toward the back-end of the garage where many of the Guardians' vehicles were parked.

Zarah let out a low whistle when she eyed the car he was approaching. A remote in his hand started the metal beauty as they reached it.

Before her sat a sleek new sports car, its black, shiny exterior shimmering beneath the dim garage lights. The windows were tinted dark, and the rims were a well-polished chrome. The low rumble of the dual exhaust reverberated throughout the surrounding concrete walls. Zarah nearly salivated as she stared at the powerful car. She didn't care that she was clueless to the model, or other manly stuff like horsepower. All she wanted was to get behind the wheel and fly down a straight strip of highway.

Still standing beside her, he frowned.

"No, you can't drive it," he said harshly as if he had read her thoughts. Of course, they could read each other's thoughts, but many of them didn't unless it was necessary. Most held up mental blocks to prevent it. Most never worried about it. She certainly didn't want anyone reading through her thoughts though, afraid of the dark things they would find there. If they saw the things she'd done, they would hate her more. Quickly shaking her worry, she turned back to Draven and played it off. She knew he hadn't truly read her thoughts that time; he'd only made the comment from sheer observation at her admiration of the car. Her prolonged silence and paranoia though could lead him into suspicion and that was the last thing she'd want.

She stared at him in mock horror, placing a hand on her chest.

"Oh, you just broke my heart!" She acted melodramatic, dropping her jaw open, and faking a sad attempt at a lip tremble that she'd once seen a girl do on television. The corners of his mouth perked slightly, twitching, as if he was fighting off a chuckle. She could see in his eyes he was not going to let himself get comfortable with her, despite that she was actually trying to show some humor. He still was going to hate her either way.

"Let's just go," she finally said. Her light mood turned bleak again as obligation set in.

 Three

The Rogue snarled and hissed as they approached it. Zarah was on one side, Draven on the other. The two of them had surprisingly made a decent team throughout the night—already having slayed three others earlier. They hunted well, picking up scents. Toward the end of the night, the Guardians found themselves on the roof of a building where they'd picked up heavy activity. The one they were cornering then held a human in his grasp. Luckily, the young man was still alive. Zarah kept her gun aimed at the Rogue, while Draven reached forward to grab the creature.

With a single swipe, Draven and the out-of-control Vampire were immediately in a scuffle. The creature temporarily forgot his meal in order to fight for his life. The human was tossed to the side like a ragdoll. A Rogue's speed was generally a bit faster than that of a Guardian or Hider's because they fed much more frequently.

This one was exceptionally fast because of his newer status. He was an old Vampire, but a younger Rogue, and this made it a bit harder to get a hold of to take down. He had two advantages on his side—being a Rogue, and the age. He ran at astounding speeds in circles around the roof, blurring his image. Zarah or Draven couldn't get a clear shot.

Draven was thrown into a nearby metal vent, and the Rogue turned to face Zarah, who was trying to get the unconscious human away from the scene. It leapt, flying across the length of the building, and landed in front of her. She tried aiming her gun to shoot, but wasn't fast enough as the creature reached forward and slapped it out of her hand. It soared high in the air above their heads before landing at the edge several feet away.

He shoved her into a brick wall, and she winced when her back slammed hard into the building. The roof door was nearby, but being an abandoned building, it was probably locked with no way to get inside. She quickly recovered, baring her fangs with rage and hissing. Draven was on his feet again and heading back into the scene when more trouble appeared. As he started to approach to help Zarah, another Rogue dove on to his back causing him to shout out in surprise.

"There's two, Zarah!" he screamed, beginning to struggle with a female Rogue on his back. He made a few small maneuvers to keep her from biting him. Her snapping was loud, and everything became a blur as the two struggled.

Zarah looked over at her partner, distracted momentarily by the confusion. It was unusual to see two Rogues fighting together. They were normally loners.

Her attention was captured again when the male Rogue grabbed her arm, pulling her up against his body.

"Do you not recognize me, Zarah?" His voice came out in a deep baritone, ridiculously normal and familiar from a long time ago. She stopped struggling against his grip and stared at him wide-eyed. Thick, wavy blonde hair that reached down over his ears, tall and a lean-muscled build, almond-shaped eyes and a strong jaw line...and the unmistakable hard-edged deep, raspy voice. She realized instantly who he was and began to stutter.

"T-Thomas?" she asked in disbelief.

That small amount of shock and hesitation could have cost her life. With a nod, the creature smiled mischievously and pushed her away from him. He stopped attacking and motioned for the female Rogue to stop as well. Draven was stunned when she obeyed and backed away from their fight. He glanced over at Zarah with a confused frown.

Zarah peeked out of the corner of her eye to see the human still unconscious. Inspecting him quickly, she noticed no bite marks and secretly sighed in relief.

"The human is unharmed. I only brought him here to get your attention," Thomas said. Slowly, she began to reach for another gun that was snug in the holster on her hip.

"I wouldn't if I were you."

"And why the hell not?" she growled, her hand still placed on the gun, prepared to draw it and begin shooting. It was her chance at taking him down. She'd been waiting for this opportunity. He remained still, nodding his head briefly toward Draven.

"If you do, Alyssa certainly won't mind turning your partner Rogue before you could attempt to pull the trigger again. We all know it only takes one small bite," he answered, eyebrows raised with interest to see what Zarah would do. She narrowed her eyes and glanced between the two Rogues, noting the positions. Alyssa, the female that had arrived on the scene, still stood dangerously close to Draven, who was unarmed after the struggle. They stood several feet away, near the edge of the roof. She looked back to Thomas' scarlet eyes and nodded, slowly taking her hand away from the holster, holding it up in defense.

"Good girl. Now we can talk." Thomas smirked. Zarah looked past him toward Draven and clenched her jaw in anger.

"What do you want, Thomas?" She brought her focus back to him.

"I just want to talk."

She sighed in defeat, but kept her body tensed, prepared for more fighting. This was an unusual scenario, and she couldn't help but to be confused by it.

"You're intelligent," she noted, eyeing him with suspicion.

Thomas let out a dark chuckle and nodded.

"You think that just because I'm a Rogue, I'm completely lost to the world and unable to communicate?"

"Rogues *are* lost. Once a Vampire is gone to the bloodlust, all previous intelligence is gone, and the only thing lived for then is sustenance," she remarked angrily.

"That is what we have been trained our whole lives!"

"Oh? Like how you suddenly were cured?" he asked with a mock tone, raising an eyebrow. She growled, her fangs glinting in the moonlight.

"I am cured," she hissed.

"Perhaps," he started. "But I can imagine you still hear that dark voice at the back of your mind every so often."

She stared at him in silence, refusing to respond. There wasn't a chance she'd let him get to her. Thomas was her past—and Draven was witnessing this sweet little reunion.

"I'm not your problem, Zarah, and we didn't entice you here to kill you. There are things you're not aware of," he continued when she didn't say anything.

"Like what?" Draven asked, his voice laced with a mixture of curiosity and anger.

"I'm not speaking with you, Guardian." Thomas turned around and growled. The wind picked up, sending a chill through the late night air. The two Guardians and two Rogues were staring at each other, tension clear in everyone's eyes.

In the distance, sirens sounded in the city. Longview, Texas wasn't the cleanest of places as it once had been. Now growing overcrowded through the years, and full of crime amongst the humans, she'd seen many changes in her own time. She had a feeling she was going to continue seeing more as the country continued on its path of expanding cities while the population rose and with that, violence. The humans were a strange species themselves. Shouts could be heard from somewhere below the building on the street, and Zarah picked up the scent of smoke and fire.

"Okay, Thomas. You have my attention for now. What are you trying to tell me?" she finally spoke with a frown. He smiled.

"Guardians need to be more careful. You're being fed lies."

"What kind of crap is that?" she snapped, taking a step toward him, once again reaching for her gun. Out of the corner of her eye, she saw Alyssa grab Draven's arm, bringing his wrist dangerously close to her mouth. Zarah took a deep breath to calm her anger, and let her hand drop from the holster again. Once Thomas saw she was not going to attack, he made a motion at the female, and she dropped Draven's arm. Draven rubbed his wrist where the woman's strong grip had held and then met Zarah's eyes with fury.

"I mean Rogues are evolving, Zarah. We're not all completely mindless killing monsters like you're being taught. Sure, a lot of the species is.

But not all." Thomas appeared controlled, sincere. She saw honesty in his features and swallowed back her nagging troubles. He took a risk to seek her out, and after witnessing a few of her own weird events with other Rogues while hunting, she knew something wasn't right.

"You know I'm telling the truth. Think about your hunt last night."

She swallowed. Had Thomas been following her? Apparently. He knew about the Rogue she had killed the previous night—the one that she had heard speaking, conscious and intelligent. She shook her head in disbelief.

"How? How did your kind get like this?" she asked.

"Some Vampire made an elixir to better control our desires. He fed it to a Rogue, and then every vampire he bit after that or vampires that were bit by the conscious ones, became like him. Intelligent, controlled. I don't know all the details exactly," he explained. She furrowed her brows and looked over at the human.

"You call that being controlled? Still taking

humans to kill?" She held an angry accusation while staring at the unconscious human laying nearby.

"That was merely bait. You wouldn't object to the death of a child molester, would you?" He blinked before a slow smirk spread across his face.

"I found that fool trying to rape a thirteen year old girl."

Zarah narrowed her eyes and tried to access his thoughts. Images and voices swirled together and she saw Thomas wasn't lying about the human. He had found the man on the first floor of the same abandoned building they were on about to force himself on a young girl. Alyssa had led her home while Thomas knocked the man out and carried him up to the roof. When she pulled away from his thoughts, Zarah stared at him in shock.

"The sun will be up soon. You two should get back to the Compound," he told her before glancing over at Draven. Zarah nodded.

"I don't understand though, Thomas, why

would you tell us this?"

"This guy has big nasty plans. I don't know what yet, but we would like to help figure this all out with you."

Draven remained quiet, but Zarah could clearly see the anger working its way through his features. His jaw was set; his normally bright blue eyes were clouded and stormy. And with what she was about to do, she'd never live it down from him.

"Okay," she said, agreeing to work with the two Rogues. There was definitely something unusual going on, and she had every intention of finding out what. No matter what it took.

"Good. We'll find you again soon." Alyssa approached then, taking his hand in hers as they turned to walk away from the scene. Zarah stared at the young woman, remembering her from before also. She hadn't known Alyssa had sacrificed her life to be with Thomas until this night. Her disappearance had never been discussed before.

Draven walked over to Zarah, staring down at her furiously.

"You're just going to let them go?" he asked in a low growl. His voice came out in a husky whisper, the accent winding harshly around the vowels.

"Yes, Draven. I intend to find out what is going on. He wasn't lying. I could tell," she replied with a simple nod.

"Thomas!" she suddenly called out. He stopped, turning his body slightly to look back at her. Alyssa tensed beside him, waiting.

"You do know that I will still kill you one day, right?" There wasn't any joke in the question, but a fact...a statement that was left hanging in the fogged air as if this had been said before.

He smirked and nodded.
"Of course, Zarah. And I certainly look forward to dying by your hand."

The two disappeared over the ledge, leaving the Guardians on the roof alone.

Draven turned to Zarah and looked down at

her in confusion.

"Who was that anyway?" he asked curiously. She should have known he'd ask. She dreaded answering, bringing back the memories that she tried to tuck away and forget.

"Thomas?"

When he nodded, awaiting her response, she pulled her gaze from his and stared straight ahead, out over the city. The breeze ruffled her hair lightly, and the air had grown colder in their time up there. She sighed sadly.

"He was my brother."

Four

The sun began to rise in the distance as Draven sped through the downtown streets to get back to the Compound. Zarah gripped the door handle tightly at each sharp turn he made, the tires screeching cries around the curves. She glanced over at him briefly, the light on the dashboard illuminating his face. He looked both furious and determined. Angry at what occurred on the rooftop, adamant to get back before the sunlight burned them to ash.

She watched him accelerate even more when the light of the sky began to grow brighter behind them. They weren't far from the base and if they could make it into the garage in time, Zarah knew they would be safe. Thinking about the hues of orange and pink chasing them, she dared a look backward only to be met with pain in her eyes, causing her to let out a hiss and turn back to the front. Her reaction made Draven glimpse over at her momentarily as she covered her face with her hands and slide farther down in her seat.

Zarah felt the familiar bump of the garage entrance when Draven raced into the dark concrete parking garage but continued keeping her hands over her face. Her eyes burned from the flash of light that had hit them. She knew she would be okay though. When he came to a stop, parking the car at the farthest, darkest corner of the parking area, she remained still, taking deep breaths to calm herself through the pain.

After a few minutes, she began to feel lighter and cooler, her eyes only mildly stinging. Pulling her hands away, she slowly looked up. Draven continued to sit there quietly, staring straight ahead at the gray wall he had parked in front of.

"Are you okay?" he finally asked, breaking the awkward silence. Zarah didn't hear any concern in his voice, only its usual rough, cold edge.

"Yeah," she muttered, pulling the seat belt off and getting ready to climb out of the car.

"Nice driving, by the way," she added, though her tone was sarcastic.

"Wait, Zarah." He reached out his hand to quickly grab her arm and demanded her stay seated in the car.

"We have to talk."

She let out an exasperated sigh and glared over at him with impatience. All she wanted to do was get inside, splash water in her eyes, and take her rest. She didn't want to sit out there having a discussion with him, knowing well enough that the talk would just lead into them fighting anyway.

"Can't it just wait?"

"No. I want to know what is going on right now. Did you let Thomas go because he is your brother? Or did you let him go because you really believe what he was saying? Either way, both are crazy moves on your part."

It was obviously bothersome. A vein was

popping out in his forehead from frustration and she restrained from snapping back.

"I don't want to argue about this right now," she growled, pulling her arm out of his grip. She wasn't exactly on friendly terms with him anyway, so he didn't have the right to know about her past.

"Well, I do," he replied through clenched teeth, leaning across the center console and staring at her. She hated it when he stared at her like that.

"Either you tell me what is going through your crazy little head about this, or I tell Nathanial that you failed miserably tonight and let two Rogues go. Plus I will tell him about their intelligence and other such interesting facts. He probably would be fascinated in that, don't you think?"

Zarah glared silently at Draven, her eyes narrowed with fury.

"I told you. I believe what Thomas says. Something is going on, and it is our duty to find out. You saw for yourself that those two were different."

When she answered, her voice came out cautious and soft, trying to refrain from yelling at him.

"I think the information needs to be kept away from Nathanial for now, at least until we find out what this is about."

"Fine. I'll go with this… for now… But, one wrong move from either of you, and I won't hesitate to shoot." He didn't say if he'd just shoot the pair of Rogues or include her, too.

Draven jumped out of the car and slammed the door. She climbed out slowly to see that he still stood near the car, waiting for her. He was only there so that he could hit the lock button on his car remote. The chirp of the car as he pressed it announced that the alarm was set. They walked beside each other to the elevator in silence. Zarah had nothing to say about his remark. If he was right and she was wrong, she'd want him to shoot her anyway.

"I've been worried about the two of you! The

sun has been up for half an hour now," Nathanial said when they stepped into the Compound.

"Everything okay?"

"Everything is fine. We were held up a bit longer than expected, but made it back into the garage before the sun hit us at least," Draven responded before Zarah could. She looked over at him, shock sparkling through her eyes. It appeared he wasn't telling Nathanial what had actually happened and that pleased her. Glad that he was keeping his word, she nearly let out a breath of relief.

Nathanial glanced over the both of them, his eyes stopping on Zarah as worry creased his brows. Now that she was in a well-lit area, she could see from a nearby mirror that the skin surrounding her eyes were a deep pink from the mild burns.

"You tried to look back at the sun when it was too close. You should know by now that you can't do that, Zarah," Nathanial chided. She looked down at her feet in shame and nodded.

"Get some rest. There'll probably be another busy night ahead of you, I'm sure. I don't want to see you back so late next time though. That makes me worry too much," Nathanial instructed the both of them before walking away.

Zarah rubbed around her eyes gently with her hands and began heading down the hall toward her apartment. She didn't bother saying anything to Draven, and didn't even realize that he was following her until she reached the door of her room and heard him clear his throat.

"Put a cold, wet rag over your eyes while you sleep," he suggested. "That should help."

"Are you suddenly pretending to be my friend?" she asked sarcastically, placing her key in the lock and turning the knob. She opened the door, flipped a light switch on the wall nearby, and then turned back to face Draven with a frown.

"Or do you have something else you're trying to say to me?"

He looked down at her, his lips pressed in a

thin line, his jaw slightly clenched as if he were trying to suppress his usual angry mood. For an odd moment, she wondered what it'd be like if they actually were friends before dismissing that thought completely with a foul taste in her thoughts.

"No, I was just trying to be helpful." he shrugged and began to turn away.

"See you tonight."

Zarah watched his retreating back from the doorway, her head tilted slightly in shock and confusion at his sudden mood change. When he disappeared around the corner, she stepped back into her room and closed the door.

Within a short time, Zarah had showered and was lying in her bed with the lights out and a cold rag over her eyes. She found getting much sleep difficult though, and the ticking of the wall clock wasn't helping matters any. Thomas' face kept flashing in her mind. She knew that he'd been Rogue, but had secretly hoped to never meet up with him again no matter how long she'd been casually looking out for him.

That night was strange...seeing Thomas with his mate, Alyssa, both of them seemingly normal. If it hadn't been for the wild red eyes, she would have never known they were Rogue. However, something wasn't right, and she knew it. Zarah was determined to find out what was going on within the Rogue community, and why the species were suddenly turning back into intelligent, controlled creatures. It was evident that they still killed to survive, they were still lost to the bloodlust, but there was an unusual change taking place.

As Zarah slowly and finally began to drift off into sleep, her mind filled with past memories of the dealings with her brother.

Six months prior to her going Rogue, she was a Guardian at the Compound with Thomas. He was one of the elite—the Vampire that you didn't cross in a fight. They had been partnered together when Rogues became larger in numbers—an "infestation", Nathanial had called them—and she had always enjoyed fighting alongside him.

One night in particular, however, tore the two apart, and nothing had been the same since.

"Zarah! We've been trapped!" Thomas yelled as he ran forward to stand beside her. Her eyes scanned the area around them, and she could see with clarity he had been right. There were dozens of Rogues surrounding them in that abandoned back parking lot, with only the two of them to fight. There was no way they were both escaping this situation alive and she knew it. Not unless there was a miracle—and she hardly believed in those.

"Thomas...what I want you to do is run. I'll be the bait. You run and get back to the Compound as fast as you can," she whispered to him, drawing her gun out slowly. If one of them was going to die, it was going to be her. He was the Compound's finest, and he had a mate waiting for him.

"Like hell," he growled out angrily, keeping his attention alert around the both of them. He yanked two guns from his holster.

"Get ready for the fight of our lives, little

sister."

Hisses and snarls grew louder as the Rogues were approaching them. Thomas began to fire his guns. As he did, Zarah aimed and shot hers off also. The rabids were coming at them full-force. Some of the Guardians' bullets hitting a few in the head held them back. But there were still so many...and it didn't take long before they were both out of ammunition, left to fight by hand the best that they could. The bullets had taken out barely half of the crowd.

"Get out of here! Now!" Thomas screamed at her as most of the Rogues were trying to overpower him. He was the strongest between him and her. Instinctively, the species went after the strongest for recruitment providing they didn't kill him. Zarah let out a shout of protest, shaking her head, before continuing her fight with the three that were focused on her. She had a small silver dagger in her hand, and was using it well to defend herself against the Rogues. Silver was deadly to a vampire if struck through the head or through the heart. It was a slow, poisonous death.

She could hear Thomas' struggles against the number of beings that he was fighting against, and could tell he was beginning to lose energy. Zarah fought harder, slashing the dagger at the Rogues, striking one through the heart. The other two, momentarily shocked, stopped fighting and looked down at the fallen vampire, allowing her just enough time to strike out at them without hesitation.

When she heard her brother's shout of pain, the blood in her veins turned to ice. Slowly turning back to the scene, her eyes widened in horror. Thomas had managed to take all but one Rogue out during his fight. But the one remaining found the advantage quickly of her brother's tired body, and bit him. Thomas lay crumpled on the pavement, the crimson liquid flowing from his neck. Fury overtook her and she charged at the Rogue that stood above her brother with a cry of outrage. The monster wasn't phased. He reached out swiftly, hitting her with a force that sent her flying across the lot. When she recovered from the blow, she sat up and hissed, trying to get up again.

"Don't bother. He'll find you, I'm sure," the Rogue said, causing Zarah to stop and stare in shock. She had never seen one speak until then. Before she could move, the creature had her brother and disappeared somewhere within the shadows. She started shouting for her brother, punching a nearby brick wall until her fists bled. Tears fell when she realized she was going to be alone—her brother had been all the family she'd had. According to Guardian rules, he was dead once he was bitten.

She searched until the morning sun began to rise, burning her skin, before going to a Hider's community home. Ashamed and sorrowed, she refused to go back to the Compound at that time. She stayed with the Hiders for several days before returning, before going to Nathanial and relating the event.

That fight would be the last time she saw her brother, until six months later when she went Rogue herself.

The memories faded as Zarah awoke, the rag on her face no longer cold and the thirst eating at her insides.

Five

As soon as Zarah dressed, she heard a light knock on her door.

Opening it, she faced Draven. He stood there, the artificial blue-glow of the lights illuminating his features, making his pale skin stand out in contrast against his shaggy dark hair and his eyes gleam. Unlike the few other women that resided in the Compound, however, she did not 'swoon' over his appearances, no matter how handsome he actually was to her.

"Come in." Her voice remained flat as she shifted to the side and allowed him room to step inside. He nodded and took a few steps in the doorway as she closed the door behind him.

"I'm not ready yet, so you can just wait," she

explained, heading toward her small kitchen and grabbing a drink. She raised a bottle toward him, offering him a drink, but he shook his head.

"No thanks, I already had mine. Enjoy."

She nodded and began drinking while he took a seat at one of the bar stools near the counter. His smirk turned up a small corner of his mouth, lighting up his eyes with it. Zarah couldn't help but notice that if he smiled, it would probably be disastrous for any woman.

"How are your eyes?" he asked after a long silence. He was playing with one of her latest crafts on the counter: a crocheted pair of fingerless black gloves.

"Still a little sore, but better." She paused from her drink to answer him.

"You know...I didn't get much sleep because of what happened. I think I need more of an explanation. How did Thomas go Rogue? How did you go Rogue? Maybe if I understood a bit more, I could help better." He stared at her through his narrowed blue eyes. The teasing smirk was gone. His glare made her shiver.

Zarah eyed Draven warily. All of this time he made fun of her because she was once Rogue, and now suddenly he wanted to know *how* she had become Rogue. Why should she even tell him? Who's to say that he wouldn't turn on her during this mission in the end and kill her anyway? She was already embarrassed enough that he had been there to witness the reunion with her brother, that he now knew Thomas was very much alive still—despite that he was Rogue, he was the very thing they hunted nightly.

"Thomas and I were ambushed by Rogues one night when we were out hunting." Her answer was cautious and tense. She still didn't want to tell him everything. It was a matter of trust between them.

"You were both turned Rogue at the same time then?"

Zarah shook her head.

"No. Only Thomas. I fought, but in the end, I

wasn't strong enough to keep that one last Rogue off of him. Next thing I knew, they disappeared, and I was abandoned in the back of a parking lot beat to hell. I went to a Hider's Den for three days before returning to the Compound…without my brother."

"And you? How did you go Rogue eventually?" Draven leaned forward onto the counter, his voice carrying a slight rough edge. He pushed the hand-made gloves to the side carelessly and focused on her. She could tell the subject was becoming difficult for both of them, and despite that it seemed he was trying to be civil, she knew that he likely didn't feel entirely confident of her 'cure'. His clenched fists sitting on the counter in front of her spoke volumes without words that he was barely keeping his emotions under control.

Zarah looked up at the wall clock to see that it was past the usual time for them to be getting out for their rounds. To add, she really did want to try to meet up with Thomas again to find out more details of what was going on.

"That, Draven, is for another conversation.

It's time for us to go." She was thankful to end the awkward conversation.

As they headed to his car in the parking garage, he looked down at Zarah to see a distant far-away look in her eyes, and wondered what she was thinking. He refused to invade her thoughts though, and instead remained quiet. He hadn't bothered to press her for an answer or explanation to his question, figuring that if she ever felt comfortable enough to tell him how she was turned Rogue, she would tell him.

"Where to first?" he asked as he started up the engine and put it in reverse.

"How about we try and find Thomas to get some more answers?"

When he looked back over at her to agree, something caught in his throat. He didn't know what had suddenly changed…maybe it was the light of the full moon along with the blue lights of the dash glowing…but he was finding her even more beautiful than he'd ever found her before.

He'd never found her anything less than intimidating and beautiful, but it could never happen with her.

He quickly shook the thoughts forming in his mind, screaming the word, *'Tainted!'* to himself as he turned back away to face the road, noting that he was spending too much time around her and nodded. Thoughts of another matter, something that would surely infuriate her if she found out, crossed his mind. The time spent around her was affecting him, making it an underlying issue. It was something that had occurred when she had first arrived back to the Compound after curing her Rogue mind. Something extremely critical.

Perhaps he would tell her someday when he felt the time was appropriate, whether it made her angry or not, she had a right to know.

"Yeah, talking to Thomas sounds like a good idea," he grumbled sarcastically at last. His semi-good mood was gone.

As Draven began to pass the city park, Zarah

caught sight of unusual shadows, and immediately her senses perked. The movements were jerked and too-fast to be anything human, but she was definitely seeing a cluster of shapes and picking up scents through her open window.

"Stop!" she shouted, sending him to a screeching halt as he swerved the car over to the side of the road, while another car almost hit him and blared its horn in protest. She quickly slapped her head in annoyance and cursed under her breath.

"That's sneaky," she muttered in annoyance.

"Well, hell, Zarah, what do you expect when you're screaming for me to stop the car?" Draven turned and yelled. She wasn't looking at him anymore though, and silently stared out the window with a frown. Her body had become tense.

"What is it?"

She pointed quietly in the direction of the park.

"There's something going on over there. I

think we should go check it out."

Draven looked in the same direction and saw what she was talking about. Sure enough, she was right to be suspicious. It seemed there was something weird going on. The clouds opened again for the moonbeams to fall through, casting a soft blue glow and more light for them to see. Gathered in a small group, openly, were a number of Rogues…and they all seemed to be talking amongst themselves as if they were having some sort of meeting.

"Okay, let's go. Keep very quiet and try to keep our distance without being noticed. Hopefully we can still hear something." Draven opened the car door and climbed out. Zarah quickly followed behind him.

"Then we'll attack and kill them, right?" Zarah whispered as they crossed the street and crouched behind some bushes. Draven was already loading the clips for his guns when he looked down at her with a wide smile. His fangs flashed in excitement. Her breath caught, surprised at the reaction of her body from his simple expression. She'd been right earlier with her thoughts on how dangerous that smile could be.

"Then we attack and kill." He lead her gently by her elbow closer to the cluster of Rogues, where they hid behind more bushes and began listening to the conversation.

"The Commander says the woman is a walking elixir to a complete cure. Even though we are intelligent and controlled now because of his previous invention, he now claims that he can actually cure us of the rabid poison if we'd rather that," one Rogue was saying to the others.

Zarah counted at least six of them present. The one speaking seemed to be the leader of the pack.

"But of course, it's going to be for a price. We have to wait and see if we are worthy. Only the Commander will determine that. And he has instructed that whoever finds this girl and brings her to him, untouched, without a bite…will be one of the ones to get this reward," he continued.

Draven and Zarah glanced at each other. They knew who they were talking about. The Rogues were discussing Zarah, and there she was, right under their noses.

"But, why is the Commander worried about the cure? I thought he wanted us all to remain as we are so that we keep our army together?" another spoke up with hesitation.

"He's just offering the choice. If you choose the cure, you're still to remain loyal with the army. The Commander chose us for a reason to begin with. Then the ones that we've turned, we have chosen for our own reasons. We are a family. We are to stay together," the leader answered with a growl.

"He has his own secrets he is keeping from me as well. I don't know the entirety of his plans yet. I can tell you this, it will be worth sticking around."

When Zarah heard the word 'family', she thought of Thomas, her only brother, the only family she had left. Or had had left. Whatever.

Until he was stolen from her by a Rogue. And the Rogue mindset ruined it all for her.

The fury rose within her as she turned the safety off of her gun and nodded to Draven.

"I'm done listening to this; I say that we jump in now before they leave," she whispered to him.

He looked over at her to see the rage flashing in her eyes, a smirk playing on his own lips as he pulled his own from his holster and nodded. The silver of the guns flashed in the moonlight.

"Alright, Zarah, let's go kick some ass."

Before they could take a single step from their hidden spot, a hand landed hard on Zarah's shoulder, causing her to turn and hiss in defense at the dark form behind her. Draven had both of his guns aimed and ready to shoot, spinning sharply around to face whoever had crept upon them.

"Take it easy there, it's just me," the familiar gruff of Thomas' voice came out in a whisper.

Zarah took a deep breath and stared at her Rogue brother with narrowed eyes while Draven lowered his weapons.

"What are you doing here, Thomas? Are you with this group?" She looked back over to the gathered Rogues. They were still there, talking amongst themselves, unaware of the Guardians' presence. A few more had arrived since their own arrival and it seemed they were still waiting for more.

"No, but I know the leader of that pack. Actually, I've been looking for you, my dear sister. Glad I found you, too, because just when I get here, it looked like you Guardians were about to go in and commit suicide by fighting the army by yourselves," Thomas replied with a smirk.

"I thought we learned our lesson with fighting packs when you're outnumbered a long time ago."

Zarah's jaw dropped as the anger boiled over. She couldn't believe her brother would blatantly bring that up or treat her that way in front of someone else. So what if it was just Draven. It embarrassed her. It pissed her off. More importantly, the remark stung.

"We can handle ourselves just fine." Her composure snapped. Her voice came out choked, full of doubt and worry. She was a tough fighter, but maybe he was right. Even with Draven there, they were outnumbered considerably. Going in blindly would have been outrageous. She'd been doing a lot of crazy stunts since her return though.

The wind began to pick up, and they all ducked further down toward the ground quickly so that it wouldn't carry their scents over to the group. Leaves rustled nearby, causing them to jump. When a cat hopped out beside her and sauntered down the street to the next place it could dig for trash, she nearly laughed away her nerves. She loved cats even though they weren't particularly fond of her. It was a part of the whole vampire thing.

"You didn't even hear me approach because you weren't on alert, Zarah. I could have snapped your neck," Thomas hissed out beside her.

"It looks like you've got a bit sloppy and need to be back in basic training again with a maneuver like that."

Damn, it didn't matter that he was Rogue. He still sounded the same as he did when he was Guardian—as bossy and smart-mouthed as ever.

Her teeth began to grind.

"Hey, Guardian, you been working with her in the gym? I think she's slacking." He started directing his annoying commentary to Draven with mocking laughter.

She turned back to Thomas with a growl, her turquoise-amethyst eyes glowing wildly in the dark, preparing to lunge until Draven gripped her arm and pulled her back.

"That's enough," Draven ordered sternly. "Get done with the damn sibling rivalry and let's get back to the task at hand here to figure out what we're going to do."

Zarah looked over at Draven with a frown and glanced down at where his hand held her arm. When he saw her eyes flash back up to his face, he released his grip and turned his attention back to the Rogues. More seemed to have gathered around the pack since Zarah and Thomas had been sitting there bickering. They were surely outnumbered then, and she was growing more frustrated with each passing second as she remained crouched behind the large shrubbery between her Rogue brother, which was an odd case in itself, and Draven, a Guardian that she assumed only to be sticking around just because it was his job.

"The Commander will meet with us soon. We are also waiting on some others to arrive," they heard the nearby Rogue leader tell the followers.

"We should leave before they figure out we're here. Especially you, Zarah," Thomas said finally in a whisper after a long silence passed between them.

"I want to see who this 'Commander' is at least first," Zarah said through clenched teeth, gripping the butt of her gun so tightly that her knuckles turned even whiter.

"Zarah," Draven started to protest, trying to take her elbow to lead her away. He was agreeing with Thomas on the situation, realizing in that moment it was beginning to look dangerous for them both as the group of Rogues were growing larger, and they didn't have the backup to help them if a fight ensued.

"I said no. I'm staying to see who this Commander is," she turned and hissed furiously at him, causing him to drop his hand immediately.

"Fine. Just a look, and then we leave." His eyes were dark, blending against the surrounding night. There was a brief silver spark in the depths of his irises...an emotion she couldn't pick up through the rolling tide of anger. She met them with hers and hesitated briefly, staring at him as he clenched and unclenched his fists at his sides, before turning back to the scene without a response.

Voices carried roughly through the wind around them as they fell silent again. Bugs buzzed loudly in their ears and the air grew colder as the minutes passed on. They stared ahead at the group, waiting and unblinking. Finally, after several long minutes, the Rogues stopped their conversation as a cloaked figure stepped from the shadows of the trees at the far end of the park. Zarah strained her neck to get a glimpse of the being's face, but couldn't see through the heavy black hood.

"Commander, we are all here," the leader said to the robed figure. The creature in the black-hooded cloak nodded once and continued walking through the crowd of the unusual rabids toward the front where the main speaker from earlier was standing. When the robes passed the bushes of where the trio sat hiding, the being paused briefly, and slightly turned his head before continuing forward. Zarah realized she'd been holding her breath when a rush of air was released after he'd passed. Draven and Thomas looked over at her with quiet, questioning frowns. She shrugged.

When the Commander made it toward the front, he leaned forward and whispered something to the leader. The Rogue's eyes widened and intensified with fury before turning to shout out to the crowd what the Commander had just said.

"Seems we have some spies among us!" he yelled with a crazy laugh and pointed toward the direction of where they were.

"Shit." Draven growled as Zarah inhaled sharply and readied her weapons to prepare for a possible battle. If they couldn't get away, they were going to be fighting for their lives in this one...

Insane laughter picked up through the wind as the Rogues began to head their way. Zarah could see some of them licking their lips as they crunched their feet over dead leaves. They snapped their teeth and clicked their nails together in intimidation, and others giggled maniacally in anticipation at the idea of discovering and devouring their eavesdroppers.

"Get out of here. I'll distract them." Thomas shoved Zarah and Draven. She turned to him in shock, unable to find words and began to stutter. He continued pushing her away, ignoring her protests.

"Just keep low to the ground and out of sight until you get to your car. Now go!"

"What about you?" Zarah asked in a rush, surprised at the worry found in her voice.

"I'll be fine, Zarah. You're forgetting, I'm one of them." He rolled his eyes.

"Get out of here. I'll find you again another

night."

She didn't argue when Draven pulled her by her arm and began to lead her in a rush back to the car. They ran with an increased speed, bent low at their waists to keep from being seen, and didn't look back at the park until they were back inside the vehicle, speeding toward the Compound.

Zarah stared out of the passenger side window. The night was barely half gone and still early. But the time wasn't really what had been on her mind. It was Thomas. She actually found herself worrying about him, hoping that he was okay at the park after he had volunteered to stay behind with that pack of Rogues. After a few minutes, she shook the thoughts and assumed that he would be fine. Just as he said, he was one of them…and he knew that pack leader. Why should she care anyway?

When they were safely back inside the Compound's garage, Draven parked but didn't move from his seat. Zarah looked over at him in confusion.

"Aren't you getting out?" She had her hand on the door handle, staring at his profile in the dim lights of the car's interior. His hair had fallen from its normally neat ponytail, and hung around his face. Oddly, she found herself admiring him. His height took a lot of the space in the small sports car. She looked at his hands in his lap—not very soft-looking, but worked. They were probably a little rough. Her thoughts began to take some weird turns and she had to quickly shake them, mentally slapping herself.

"Not yet. Sit here with me for a while. It's still early anyway." He turned the radio on and switched to a loud, heavy rock station. She frowned briefly, but let her hand fall from the door and leaned back into the seat again.

"We could have been killed out there, Zarah." Draven said in a low, calm tone after a long silence when the song ended and the station went to commercials. She sighed, knowing that she should have expected the conversation to come up.

"And you could have just left me there with

Thomas. You hate me so much. You're determined that I'm still a Rogue in disguise. This doesn't have to be your mission." She was starting to ramble, looking everywhere except at him.

"I lied."

Zarah stopped talking, turning to face him as he said those two small words. His cerulean eyes glowed at her in sorrow through the dark interior of the car. Her breath left her momentarily. She grew confused.

"Lied about what?" Her words were slow; her mouth became dry.

"Believing you're still Rogue. I just give you a hard time about that. I'm not going to sit here and say that I don't think you're tainted, though. I'd never feed from you. However, I saw for myself those months ago you fight against the urges of bloodlust."

As he explained, she could only stare at him in shock with a slacked jaw.

"You saw?"

"Those humans before you were picked up? You were weeping…you were trying to revive one…" he replied.

"You kept screaming for help."

The memory haunted her. It was a nightmare she had often.

Blood was splashed upon the walls and stained the white carpets as the color of her destruction stood out around her and three bodies lay at her feet. Yet, even through the strong metallic odor of her food source that her raging bloodlust had overpowered her for, she could faintly pick up the scents of jasmine and lilies…and just before she collapsed to the white-scarlet floors in tears, she had seen the beautiful array of flowers. They had been neatly arranged in vases across the room, sitting on the table, but even those beautiful white buds were stained with spots of the crimson fluid that she had murdered for…

"No…" It was a soft whisper at first that had escaped her lips, something that had sounded so

foreign and distant. That couldn't possibly have been her voice? There was a bright flash of lavender light momentarily. It blinded her, causing her to fall. She felt the blood on her hands, smelled it in her hair. Bile rose into her throat and she spilled the contents of her stomach onto the floor beside one of the mangled bodies. How was that possible? When was the last time she had vomited? Perhaps as a child, but shockingly, there she was for the first time in years, retching until her insides cramped.

"No." A little louder the second time, and she found it was her. She was staring at her destruction, the awful crime she'd committed. She needed help. Could someone help her? What had she done?

"NO!"

"Help!"

The floor was sticky and cold. But she lay there, screaming and crying, hitting that dead human man over and over.

And just as Draven had mentioned, she'd

cried for help, screaming until her voice was raw as she also tried to administer CPR on one of the humans.

Zarah knew now that it wouldn't have worked, not after her destruction. She had drained them. But she had been so emotionally disturbed, she didn't know. Her mind had been foggy through all of those moments. Pain had ripped through her chest and head. Her cries drowned the silent night, and then the door of that apartment burst open.

"How do you know about that?" she asked barely above a whisper.

"Nathanial was the only one that came to me."

"No, he wasn't. I was there for 'just-in-case' purposes. When it was determined that you weren't a threat, you were sedated, and I carried you out," Draven said as her eyes widened. He smirked.

"No lie."

His body had turned toward hers, and in the small space, it felt too intimate. She began to feel a little uncomfortable, backing up against the door as far as she could.

"Why are you telling me all of this?" She was suspicious, narrowing her eyes.

"Well, I'm trying to tell you that I can't abandon you during this mission, or any mission for that matter. That night, once we were sure you were stable, Nathanial made me do something," he began.

Zarah was nervous, her hands shook as they gripped the edge of the seat tightly and she stared over at him with wide eyes.

"What?"

"He made me seal a Bonding Pact with you." His answer was nonchalant, emotionless.

Zarah leapt from her seat and left the car, running into the Compound without looking back. She couldn't hear any more, couldn't respond to that. The look on her face before her departure said more than enough. She was beyond angry. She was hurt. Draven leaned forward and banged his head into the steering wheel out of frustration. He didn't try to stop her.

As he climbed out of his car, he couldn't help but wonder if he had done the right thing or not by telling her that information. Before getting into the elevator to go down to the main level, he'd determined that he had.

Seven

Zarah couldn't believe it.

A Bonding Pact? She didn't need a damn Bonding Pact, much less one with Draven. Those things were lethal. They killed. There was too much attachment involved; it was a sacred blood bond usually done between mates. And how could Nathanial talk him into doing that in the first place? In order for one to be made, he had to have signed some unbreakable contracts and fed her from his vein...but she didn't remember taking from Draven. Then again, the night she had come out of her Rogue status, she was out of it—sedated and blanked out for several days. She didn't remember much of anything after having the breakdown in the humans' home, except waking up in the hospital wing of the Compound, newly awakened and feeling what she'd guess she'd call normal again.

So, was that why Draven had been around her so much, constantly aggravating and pissing her off since her return? Because the Bonding Pact made it hard for him to keep too far away from her and that made Draven angry? Why hadn't Nathanial told her? And was that why he'd paired them up, despite knowing that they were the Compound's finest and it would be a great loss to the team should something happen to them?

Question after question raced through Zarah's mind as she continued pacing. She was back in her room at the Compound, having raced off from the parking garage after receiving the news. Tears flowed, warming her cheeks. Reaching up to swipe them away, she scowled over the weakness of her emotions.

Betrayed.

She felt betrayed by them all.

A soft knock sounded at her door. She could smell him on the other side.

Her own emotions were traitors as a mixture of overwhelming desire and hatred filled her at the same time. She let out an angry huff and wiped at more tears. His scent smelled of rich, dark masculine spices mingling with light hints of cherry. The aromas each individual carried were unique to themselves and used as a hunting maneuver when preying on humans. Guardians no longer hunted humans and hadn't since blood banks began.

"Go away, Draven." She started shedding her jacket and weapons, refusing to open the door.

"I don't want to talk to you."

"I figured that. I was just making sure that you were here."

Zarah stormed across the room and swung the door open to meet his face, not caring that he was going to see the tear tracks on her cheeks.

"You just lied again. You knew I was here, asshole. Or did you already forget that you just told me that you have a Bonding Pact with me?" Her fangs caught in the light as she bared her teeth at him. With his confession, she knew he could find her anywhere. There was a blood-bond connection between them.

Draven clenched his jaw and stared down at her darkly.

"I don't like it any more than you do, bitch. But I did my job; it's what I had to do and you could at least show some appreciation that I even told you. Nathanial wanted to keep it from you indefinitely."

She shook her head in disbelief.

"Why?" she asked.

"To keep you safe. But now, whether you know or not, you're not safe. So I figured I should tell you. It was your right to know anyway."

As he started to turn and walk away from her, she stepped into the hallway and grabbed his arm to stop him.

"No. Why did you do it? Why did you let Nathanial talk you into the Bonding Pact?" she asked again with a frown.

"In my state of mind, you could have been turned Rogue that night."

"I didn't let your teeth touch my skin," he started, cutting her off.

"And I was the only one around. He wanted a Guardian to have a Bonding Pact with you because you were curing. It was the miracle of our race; it was a big deal at the time and he kept blabbering about you being special just like he thought you were. I didn't understand. He didn't get into details. I couldn't let him down, so I agreed, and did my job."

With that final explanation, he brushed her hand from his arm and stalked away to his room. She heard his bedroom door slam down the hallway from her own before going back into hers.

She looked briefly around her quiet room before grabbing her pistol and walking out again. This wasn't the time for crochet or art or reading.

"Hey, Zarah, are you and Draven getting along alright?" She heard Nathanial ask as he came up beside her. She continued down the long, winding hallway of the Compound, her boots echoing on the polished tile, the gun still gripped by her right hand. Her boss frowned as he glanced down to see it there instead of in its holster. There was a strict Compound policy to keep weapons holstered in the halls or off-duty. She usually ignored the policies and rules, and Nathanial never seemed to reprimand her for it.

She nodded and glimpsed at him through the corner of her eyes. He had no idea that she knew anything about the Bonding Pact, and for a short moment, the rage flared again in the pit of her stomach that he'd kept such a secret. Still, she remained quiet and kept walking.

"Where are you going in such a hurry?" He sounded agitated, his steps on the rushed side as he tried to keep up with her quickening pace. She wasn't in the mood to be near him, yet he continued following.

"The shooting range," she said, making a turn and heading toward a set of large, steel double doors.

"I need to let off some steam and shoot something."

Nathanial stuttered, trying to speak. She ignored him, and pushed her way into the gym. She closed the doors, leaving him in the hallway flustered and speechless at her attitude. Sure, she'd have to hear a lecture later, but she wasn't going to concern herself about it then. On the other side of the large room was a heavy door that led to the shooting range. To get there, she'd have to cross the work-out area, and that included a few other residents who were in there at the time doing their training. The gym consisted of various weight benches, punching bags, targets for knife throwing, balance beams, and ugly bright blue wrestling mats. Walking briskly, she crossed the room and headed for the small, closed-in shooting range. From the tiny door window, she saw it was empty and let out silent breath of relief.

A few Guardians were working out but, as always, they ignored her. She could still feel their stares when she passed. One let out a fake cough.

After stepping inside, she headed for one of the small cubicles while loading her gun with lead bullets. When they practiced there was no need to use their good silver bullets. Those were made by a resident, and always limited. The practice ammunition could be store bought. Placing the blue headphones over her ears, she fired single rounds at the paper targets in front of her. The tension coursing through her body eased. Each shot relaxed her more. Her shoulders drifted down, her legs took a wider stance. The cold metal of her weapon comforted her. She let her hair down from its ponytail, the dark auburn tresses falling to her waist, and pulled up the corners of her mouth into a smile as she took a few more deep breaths and a few more shots—hitting her marks perfectly.

After replacing the targets three times, she grew tired and decided to leave. The practice helped clear her mind and ease the tension. Holstering the gun, Zarah walked slowly and relaxed back to her room. Nathanial was nowhere to be seen.

Zarah continued to calm her nerves later by stepping into the shower. The hot steam hit her skin and she took long, deep breaths as she stood still, hanging her head under the spraying water, and losing sense of time. She only stepped out when it started to grow cold, causing little goose bumps to appear on her slender arms as she turned the nozzle off, and reached for her towel around the white vinyl curtain.

Putting on a long, black silk nightgown with a matching robe, she brushed her hair while using the dryer. She opened a bottle of blood as she stepped into her small kitchen. The sweet, metallic flavor danced merrily over her tongue and down her throat, reminding her of how thirsty she'd been. Gulping down the drink, she emptied the bottle. Gasping in satisfaction, she gripped the countertop to steady herself. She wiped her mouth with a towel before rinsing out the bottle. Her gaze was momentarily hypnotized by the swirling mixture of blood and water in her sink. She stood, unblinking, watching until the water ran clear. Cold blood stolen from the humans' banks wasn't as filling as a warm-blooded donor, but this was the way it had to be. It was safe. It kept them from turning rabid.

Rogues came to be centuries ago through the means of draining humans, most times accidentally, and the constant desire for more. They went wild with bloodlust after a draining. Later, during the Plague, they evolved with a poison found in their saliva that passed along to others when bitten. Rabid vampires became weapons in themselves. One bite, human or vampire, and the Rogue virus took over in a matter of hours. Some believe it was because the Rogues fed on Plague-diseased victims that created the poison they now carry. Now they're an infestation themselves.

Zarah stared down at the empty bottle and sighed. Satisfied, but not full. That was all she would ever be. She discarded the bottle, disgusted with herself.

A while later when she climbed in bed, her phone rang.

"Hello?" she said quietly as she lay in the dark. She hadn't bothered checking her Caller I.D. to see who it was.

"Well, hello, little sister."

Zarah sat up when she heard Thomas' voice, pulling her phone briefly away from her ear to see that the number he was calling from was private.

"Thomas? Are you okay?" The silence had been awkward, filled by a mild static noise. She still didn't know exactly how to speak to him.

"I'm fine. I told you not to worry about me. But somehow I knew you still would anyway and that's why I called. Get some rest. I'll see you soon," he said, hanging up before she could respond.

Laying back down, it took her awhile before she could fall asleep as so many different thoughts continued to race through her mind.

#

That evening, she didn't feel up to doing much for the first time in years. She just wanted to stay in bed and not have to face anyone. As nice as it sounded, with the comfort of her thick covers and fluffy pillows surrounding her, she knew she couldn't. Especially when a loud knock sounded at her door, causing her to groan in annoyance. She threw a few of the decorative pillows at the door. The black velvet flew end over end and gold tassels spun around each other, before making soft thuds and landing on the floor. She heard his amused laughter on the other side before she was up. She smelled him, noting that his scent seemed even better than he has before. It caused her to let out a frustrated growl as she kicked off the covers.

Rising out of bed, she yanked her robe from a

chair and slipped it on before walking over to open the door. The tossed pillows were still in a sad pile nearby.

"That's odd. Normally you're at least dressed by now," Draven said as he eyed her appearance. She certainly had that fresh just-climbed-out-of-the-bed look going, her fangs more elongated than usual because she needed another drink, and her hair was in a disarray. But for the first time, he was seeing the softer side of her. The side outside of the heavy combat boots, ripped jeans, and fighting gear while she stood in front of him wearing a long, silk robe and barefoot with her hair down. He couldn't help but to find it…lovely, actually. His own thoughts shocked him.

"So, are you going to stand there and mock me all night, or you going to come in and wait while I get ready?" she asked, cutting in through his thoughts. Her nose scrunched up as she frowned. If she'd been human, they would say she wasn't a morning person. She was always grouchy when first waking up. Most particularly, she'd been in a foul mood with *him* in general.

"I'll be in the Lounge. Just come get me when you're done." He forced a friendly smile before turning to walk away. She nodded and closed the door, happy that he hadn't come in after all. She would have hated trying to get dressed in her small bathroom.

When she was ready, she headed to the Lounge to find Draven sitting in one of the plush recliners casually reading a human newspaper. He looked up when she approached, and motioned for her to sit in the chair beside his. She shook her head and began impatiently tapping her foot.

"No time to sit and read a silly paper. We're already running late for duty. Let's just go." She started to head out without bothering to wait for him to follow. Draven stood and tossed the paper on a nearby table.

"Zarah, are you okay? Look, I'm sorry about—" he started while they were on their way out to his car. She raised a hand to stop him in mid-sentence.

"I don't want to discuss it, Draven."

"Zarah!"

They both heard a female shout as they reached the car, causing them to stop and turn to face the source of the voice. It was Ash, one of the Compound staff members, running to catch up.

"What's up?" Zarah asked in confusion.

"I'm sorry, but I needed to give you a message before you left. Nathanial requests your presence in his office for a meeting after your shift is over," she said.

"Alright, tell him that we'll be there." She couldn't help but wonder at the back of her mind what it could be about. Why hadn't he just paged them? She reached up and double-checked her earpiece. It was on and connected.

"He would have paged, but he said he had to be somewhere. Told me to catch you, sorry. Not

Draven. Just you," she explained before she walked back toward the Compound entrance, leaving Zarah even more confused and curious than before. She looked over at Draven, who shrugged, and then climbed into his car.

The night was slow for them as they drove around searching and waiting. For a while, Draven parked the car across the street from the park again, and they sat there in silent hopes that perhaps a Rogue or two would come along for a meeting or something. But there was nothing. Only silence between the two of them and calm, still air outside that didn't reveal any scents or signs of the Rogues' presence.

"You can't give me the silent treatment all the time, you know," Draven finally said in frustrated exasperation, looking over at Zarah. His hand landed hard against the steering wheel with a slap to show his annoyance. One look though was enough to make him stare for longer than he should have. Her dark auburn hair and pale skin stood out against the dash lights. She didn't look like a monster. He always scoffed at the human vampire myths. They assumed their kind had to be pale and corpse-like. Just looking at him or Zarah would prove them wrong. She was lively. He wasn't ghastly pale.

"I can do whatever I damn well please," she replied, staring out the passenger window toward the park, not bothering to meet his gaze. He sighed loudly and shook his head.

"Fine. Well, it looks like we're not getting any action tonight, so I think we should just head back to base and you can have your little meeting with Nathanial," he said, starting the car again. She nodded in agreement, placed the safety back on her guns, and holstered them.

When they arrived back to the Compound, she didn't say anything to Draven and simply headed straight to Nathanial's office. Without even knocking, she barged in and took a seat.

"You wanted to see me?" Her eyebrows were raised with interest. She looked around briefly at his décor. He always was old-fashioned and loved his expensive, plush, antique furniture and priceless art. Of course, he'd been alive for over a hundred years. He'd have time to collect a lot of the things.

Nathanial, initially shocked by her sudden appearance, cleared his throat and moved some papers aside from his desk and into a nearby drawer.

"Oh... Yes, Zarah. I was wondering if everything was okay. You didn't seem like yourself yesterday morning, and well, I'm concerned."

"I know."

"You know what?" he asked.

"About the Bonding Pact," she said, narrowing her eyes.

"Why didn't you tell me?"

Nathanial took a long, jagged breath and leaned back in his chair, staring at her in surprise. He let a few minutes go by as he gathered his thoughts before he could respond to her.

"I'm sorry, Zarah. I didn't think it was a good idea to tell you, really. Let's face it. You and Draven never have gotten along very well exactly," he started finally, rubbing his eyes with his hands in annoyance.

"Was there a particular reason why he even told you?" he continued.

"Yes," she replied, and then proceeded to tell him about the events of the last couple of days with information that Draven and her had gathered of Rogues having grown intelligent, wanting to hunt her down for the 'cure'. She left out the part of them working with Thomas though. When she finished, Nathanial stared at her in a mixture of horror and shock.

Before he could continue the conversation, Ash rushed into the office.

"There's an emergency. Mitchell was just dropped in front of the building by some Rogues; he's been seriously injured. The doctor is wheeling him down to the hospital wing now." She was panicked, causing them to jump from their chairs and rush from the room behind her when she ran back out.

When Zarah made it to the hallway of the hospital wing with Nathanial, she saw Draven, along with a few others. They stood around the gurney that held Mitchell, one of the Guardians that had been coming in from his shift, and the doctor was working frantically to get the hospital room ready for him.

He looked to have been stabbed several times in the chest and stomach, and his head had been bashed horribly. The wounds were from something silver, harmful to all vampires in various ways, and his skin was turning a bluish-gray due to the poison in his system. His injuries were not healing. She slowly approached, walking up beside Draven, and stared down at her colleague in horror. The Rogues had never done such an act before. They either turned a Guardian, or they killed one. Never have they beaten one to the brink of death, and then left him on their doorstep. This was a warning.

Draven looked over at her with a grim expression and she knew he was thinking the same thing.

In that moment, Mitchell opened his eyes and stared hard at Zarah. With the best breath he could muster, he opened his mouth and let the words fall out in a whisper. His words sounded garbled while blood pooled at the back of his throat but it didn't matter—she still understood what he was saying. He kept repeating it, going slower each time until the pain finally made him go unconscious.

"They...they told me to tell you...they're coming for you...soon."

#

"Zarah! Behind you!" Draven shouted as he continued grappling with the Rogue in front of him.

She turned in time to see two more, a male and a female, running at her, growling and leaping toward her with ease. In one fluid motion, she raised the gun and fired, hitting the male in the stomach that sent him flying backward against the brick wall of an alley building. The female hissed furiously, her eyes widening at Zarah, as they began to struggle with each other.

When the female punched Zarah, her eyes swam and blood pooled in her mouth. She could hear Draven still struggling nearby with the Rogue that he was fighting. Anger flared within her as she thought of the past few days' events, and she soon found a grip in the female's hair, yanking her away from her body, and slammed her into the wall next to the male Rogue. Twenty-four hours had passed since Mitchell had arrived at the Compound seriously injured and left lying up in the hospital wing, and now they were out trying to continue their usual duties. Zarah felt odd. A darkness consumed her as she stared at the two laying on the ground before her, sputtering through the blood. She felt sick. Her emotions were controlling her, but she didn't care at that point.

Spitting out more of her blood, she loaded her gun again and aimed it at the male. When she heard the gunshot nearby without looking up, she knew Draven had taken care of the one he'd been fighting. He would go take care of clean-up and be back shortly. She fired her pistol, the shot striking a silver bullet directly into the male's head, before turning to the female.

"What's your name, girl?" Zarah suddenly asked, her eyes dark and fierce. They were burning around the edges. Violet flashes kept coming into the peripheral of her vision. A white-hot ferocity filled her chest, and a dark, vicious voice was whispering at the back of her mind.

The Rogue was struggling to move after having been slammed into the wall a few minutes before by her.

When she looked up at her with her lips curled back in a snarl, not answering, Zarah lifted her boot and brought it down on her leg with a heavy force.

The impact caused a crunch, echoing loudly around them, and indicated that the bone had just been crushed. The female yelped. It would take a few hours for an injury like that to heal but Zarah wasn't going to let that chance happen.

"I asked you what your damn name is. Answer me! I know you can talk!" she shouted at her.

"Janice," the Rogue finally said with a pained grunt, reaching forward to grab her leg.

"Janice. Good girl. Now tell me, Janice... Do you know anything about what happened to my colleague, Mitchell? Or anything that's going on with this Rogue Army for that matter?" Zarah asked, kneeling down in front of her and pointing the gun at her face.

Janice looked from the gun to Zarah and then smiled evilly.

"Like I'm going to tell you anything, Guardian."

The rabid spit in her face and let out a high-squealed laugh. As Zarah wiped the saliva away, she clenched her jaw and stared at the creature, unblinking. Without warning, she slammed her fist into Janice's eye, unsheathed her small, silver dagger from her belt loop, and slashed the blade across the Rogue's torso. Janice screeched in pain; she had expected Zarah to just simply shoot her in the head and get her death over with quickly, but that didn't seem to be the case now.

The Guardian was going to torture her to death.

"Zarah, what the hell are you doing?" Draven

asked behind her suddenly.

"I'll meet you back at the car," she replied darkly.

Before he could respond, she slashed at Janice again with her knife. The Rogue began to laugh and cry at the same time maniacally. Zarah's eyes glowed determined and vicious against the darkness.

Draven couldn't stand to watch any longer. Shaking his head and loading his gun, he stalked up beside her as she was about to lay into the Rogue again with her knife and shoved her aside. Zarah staggered from his force.

"Draven!" Zarah screamed at him when he shot Janice in the head with a silver bullet, officially ending it for the creature.

He turned and faced her. His face was a mix of emotion, mostly fury. His eyes were steel cold. She shrank back. Her own vision cleared.

"I don't know what your problem is. You know we don't play torture games," he growled.

"Now let's get out of here."

"Well, if it isn't my two favorite Guardians," they heard Thomas say as they exited the alley. Zarah had been walking with her head down, only looking up briefly to meet Thomas' eyes.

"Have fun down there?" he asked, motioning toward the alley that they had just come out of.

"Yeah, a real blast," Draven replied sarcastically, rolling his eyes, and then stared hard at Zarah. She only shrugged her shoulders. Thomas seemed to ignore their exchange, and started walking with them.

"I figured the two of you would like to come back to my place for a bit so that we can discuss some things," he said as they all reached Draven's car. Zarah looked over at him, meeting his red eyes with slight suspicion before giving him a nod. She could sense that Draven was a little uncomfortable with that idea though.

He raised his arms up in defense when he sensed it too.

"I swear no harm is coming. It's just me and Alyssa there. You can drive, Zarah can sit in the backseat with her gun at my head the whole time if that makes you feel more comfortable. I'm sure my little sister here would love the idea of having a gun at my head anyway."

"Alright, fine. We'll go," Draven agreed, glancing down at Zarah.

The drive was as Thomas had suggested it could be. Draven was driving with Thomas in the passenger seat, and Zarah in the center of the backseat. And as exactly as expected, to keep Draven comfortable since they still weren't entirely sure on Thomas' trust level just yet, Zarah had her gun out and pointing it at his head. He directed Draven where to go, leading him to a nice area of town where some of the extravagant apartments were, before pulling them to a stop in front of one of the buildings.

When they arrived inside, Zarah looked around at her brother's apartment and snorted. She shouldn't have been surprised. He had been so much like her when he was a Guardian. His tastes hadn't changed too much as a Rogue. Everything was immaculately clean and organized. His walls in the main room were lined with bookshelves, filled with books old and new. His floors were polished and dark hardwood, and he had black leather couches and glass tables. The apartment wasn't very large, but it was big enough for Alyssa and him—providing a main sitting room, kitchen, one bathroom and one bedroom.

"What?" Thomas asked with a smirk.

"Just clean," she replied, forcing a smile. He laughed and motioned for them to sit down.

"You know me. And you're the same way," he teased back.

"So, what's going on?" Draven asked, taking a seat near Zarah on the couch. He was clearly uncomfortable, but trying to be polite. About that time, Alyssa walked in from the bedroom and nodded a greeting at the two of them, and they waved a casual hello to her in return.

Thomas strolled over and sat next to his mate, placing an arm around her shoulder. Zarah offered her a small, welcoming smile. She remembered Alyssa—a vibrant blonde who'd once had bright green eyes, and was very tall and slender like a ballerina. Thomas and she had started dating shortly after they took their residency at the Compound, about a year before he was changed.

"The army definitely wants Zarah. They seem to think if they bring her in and extract her blood, they can create some vaccine to give to our kind, to reverse us back from the Rogue status. After you left the other night, when they discovered me in the bushes, I had to pull a lie out of my ass and say that I was there because I was walking by and became curious but didn't want to interrupt," he explained.

"Well, there has to be something else they're planning other than just this. Yesterday morning, they left a tortured Guardian on the Compound doorstep," Zarah said.

Thomas narrowed his eyes. "That's never been done before."

"I know."

"You think hacking up and torturing that Rogue was going to change anything?" Draven asked then, turning to Zarah. She spun toward him and bared her fangs.

"I was doing my job, Draven."

"No, you were being Jill the Ripper back there."

Thomas' looked between the two Guardians, finally landing his eyes on Zarah.

"So, you in turn tortured a Rogue back in that alley?" he asked. She lowered her eyes and didn't respond. He laughed loudly when he sensed what she had done.

"Way to go, little sis."

"Don't encourage her, Thomas," Draven criticized with a frown.

"Let's drop it already," she snapped. What she really didn't want to get into was what had caused her to turn into that. That hadn't been her. Something just snapped.

"Look, can you just find out what the hell is really going on behind all of this or not, Thomas?" she added, looking over at him with a pleading look in her eyes.

"Of course," he said with a smile.

Ten

The ride back to the Compound was silent. The hum of the car engine drowned Zarah's thoughts and she didn't want to look at Draven's face. She could already sense he was still angry over the night's earlier events. Hell, she didn't even know what had been going through her head or why she'd acted out like that. Something had overcome her senses. The tension between them both was clear. When he pulled into the garage and parked, she took the opportunity to steal an awkward glance at him.

He was already staring at her.

With his periwinkle gaze and his jaw set firmly, the lights of the dash illuminated his features making him look much more powerful in that confined space. She couldn't help but find a deeper respect for him.

"Are you alright?" His tone held a rough edge. The Irish accent rolled out in a gorgeous rhythm, but she swallowed back the admiration. There wasn't a hint of concern in his voice, only question of her sanity in his eyes.

She nodded and reached for the door.

"If something is wrong, or going wrong, you need to address it. Even if it's not with me. And if you ever pull a torture stunt like that again unnecessarily, I'll have to report you," he added as they climbed from the car and made their way into the Compound elevator. Once again, she only nodded. From there, not another word was passed between the two of them, but she felt like she was going to explode. Her emotions flared again, differently this time, not like the malevolent ones she'd had in that alley with the Rogue. No, these involved Draven…she had disappointed him, and it hurt her to know that—she couldn't understand the building pain in her chest.

He glanced at her from the corner of his eye as they made the trip down in the elevator. She was staring straight ahead at the closed metal doors with her mouth clenched tightly shut, her body rigid. His own hard expression softened as he clearly saw the tears she fought.

"Zarah, please, I know we haven't always been on the best of terms, we can change that. We can really try to be friends...more than just partners working together," he said softly, reaching forward to pull her back when the doors opened and she made a move to step out. She turned and stared at him in silence, her eyes still brimming with tears. Her bottom lip quivered. This time, she wasn't faking like she had the first night with the car.

"Talk to me." It was a gentle whisper, and no longer angered or rough. They stepped out together into the brightly-lit front hallway of the Compound. He still held her elbow kindly in his grasp and kept his eyes on hers. She glanced briefly around them, seeing the halls were mostly empty, before turning back to face him, and swallowing the forming lump in her throat.

"Okay," she said, her voice coming out in a rasp as she struggled to form words.

He raised one solid eyebrow and waited in silence as she cleared her throat, shuffled her feet and prepared to continue. Dropping his hand from her arm, he stepped back a bit to give her some space. An odd tingling sensation rippled through her arm where his hand had been, and she secretly wished that he would return it, but shook the thought away.

"I'm scared," she blurted out after another long silence.

"I think I'm losing my control. I fear of going Rogue again. I'm scared of what's going on out there right now."

The more Zarah let out, rambling in an almost nonsensical way, the more she slowly began feeling a little bit better. All the while, Draven stood there listening intently to her words as he had promised. His face remained emotionless until she finished and she turned her eyes back up to his, fearing what kind of expression she would see. Instead she saw a soft reassuring smile and understanding.

"Well it's about time."

She frowned in confusion. "What do you mean by that?"

"You can't be fearless all the time."

Realization dawned on her. In the recent months since she had been back working as a Guardian, she had done exactly that. Acted fearless. Acted reckless. He was simply there pointing out the obvious—her recent discovery of being afraid was perfectly normal. She maintained a hard edge of control since her return. But she'd lost it to that Rogue, which was still unexplainable. Maybe it was just an act of rage—another emotion that can take over and control any species when it gets out of hand. She'd have to watch out in the future.

"You are," she accused.

"What?" he asked, obviously puzzled.

"You're fearless."

Draven laughed loudly and shook his head. Zarah frowned and crossed her arms over her chest.

"No, I'm not. Trust me. I'm scared all the time. You scare the living hell out of me."

Her jaw dropped.

"I scare you?"

"Anyone who isn't scared of you is insane." He continued laughing.

Zarah couldn't help but smile. His laugh tumbled around her. She didn't think she had ever seen him in such a light before, and it was one that she certainly wanted to remember for a long time.

When his laughter finally died down, he looked down at her with a grin.

"Want to go grab a drink in The Lounge before you go off to bed?"

She nodded slowly in agreement and began following him. It was a bit awkward when they entered The Lounge together and a few other Guardians in there looked up in surprise at the two of them. On normal terms, the only time Zarah was there was to get Draven before going to work. Other than that, she rarely socialized. No one had ever invited her for a drink, either, so the offer had shocked her.

He motioned toward two empty, plush chairs far enough away from the few people that were there, and she took a seat while he went over to the bar to get their drinks. The room was large, almost as big as the gym, filled with couches and chairs, pool tables, dart boards, a bar, and several large televisions that hung on the walls. Draven walked back over to her a few minutes later with two silver chalices in hand, handing her one, and took a seat in the chair next to hers.

"Thanks," she muttered quietly before taking a long drink from the cup. He nodded at her.

"Hey, Draven! You gonna come play a game

with us?" one of the Guardians shouted across the room from a pool table. Zarah looked over to see it was James, one of the younger ones, but like everyone, he still knew all about her. And like everyone, he avoided her like the Plague as much as possible.

At that time of morning, most of them were in bed already. So, there were only a few in The Lounge with Draven and Zarah then.

"No, man, not this time. Rain check," Draven called back at James with a friendly smile. The other Guardian returned with a grin and nodded in understanding before getting back to his game.

"You could have went over and played a game. I don't care."

He turned and looked at her, shaking his head.

"No, this time is for you. Besides, I always beat James, and it gets a little boring."

She laughed a little that time and looked down at her empty cup.

"Want another drink?" he asked.

She looked up to meet his eyes and shook her head. She glanced around briefly, seeing James and another resident whispering to each other at the pool table. They were staring at her, watching her with the empty cup. James laughed at something she couldn't hear. An uneasy feeling came over her. She shouldn't have come there.

"No, thank you. I shouldn't anyway. I think I'm just going to go to bed now."

When she stood, setting her empty cup down on a nearby table, Draven quickly downed the rest of his and stood with her. He hadn't noticed that she was uncomfortable, or the stares and whispers.

"Alright, I think I'm headed that way myself. I'll walk you." They began to head out of The Lounge and into the hallway toward their rooms. Laughter rang in her ears in the background as they exited the room and it caused her to cringe.

"Uh, thanks again, Draven."

"For what?"

"For the talk and everything."

Zarah stopped in front of her door and stared at him with a forced smile.

"No problem," he replied, leaning casually against the wall.

"I'll still kick your ass, though, if you ever try to bite me."

She laughed, and she laughed loudly, knowing that like always he had loop-holed his way into putting a joke in somewhere. He turned and looked at her with a big grin, his fangs glinting in the light.

"I like the sound of your laugh. You should do it more often." His comment caused her laughter to soften as she started to blush. No red cheeks like she'd seen on humans, but she still felt the sensation of butterflies and flattery. An odd flutter struck her. He was making her blush...

No, she couldn't like him!

"Well, good—" she started, reaching for her door.

Before she could finish, a scream pierced the

corridor, coming from the hospital wing, capturing Draven and Zarah's attention. At once, they were both rushing in that direction with their guns drawn.

"What the hell is going on?" Draven shouted at the nurse with a frown when they reached the wing. They saw her struggling against the metal door of Mitchell's room to hold it shut.

She turned and faced them with fear flashing in her eyes. Suddenly a loud bang came from inside the room and reverberated around them. They jumped in alarm and watched the nurse struggle to hold the door.

"Mitchell's awake. He's Rogue!"

"What?" Zarah and Draven asked in disbelief at the same time.

The nurse turned to them panic-stricken. It was then that they saw the blood on her uniform. Her small hands held the door tightly as possible as another rumble came from within the room, getting their attention and breaking the shock. Mitchell was trying break free, and they could hear his deep growl of frustration when he couldn't get past the steel door's lock, or the nurse that held the door on the other side.

"That can't be right." Zarah frowned.
"He didn't have any bite marks when he came in."

The nurse looked at her and shook her head.
"No, he didn't. He was injected. We didn't notice the puncture wound until this morning when we went in for the sponge bath. And that was when he woke up. The doctor…oh heaven…the doctor was in there. I barely got out…" she stuttered through tears.

Draven walked over and gently moved her aside with a reassuring smile.

"It's okay. Nothing is your fault. Why don't you go clean yourself up, and then go get Nathanial? We'll take care of this problem."

After the nurse wiped her tears away and nodded, she left the area in a hurry. Zarah looked at Draven warily before staring at the closed door that currently held Mitchell captive.

He was beating on it again, pounding his

fists and yelling. A string of muffled curse words came through. Dents protruded the metal. Draven remained silent as he checked his gun to make sure it was loaded with enough ammunition before pulling the hammer back and switching the safety off.

She did the same with her gun, stepping up beside him.

"I don't want you to shoot unless I say. He's fresh, so he should be relatively quick to take down," Draven instructed. She nodded in agreement, backing up a few steps behind him to be prepared to help him if he needed it.

Draven slowly reached forward to spring the lock, his hand on the gun's trigger. Zarah watched on intently.

As the door came open, Mitchell, the newly turned Rogue, ran forward with a snarl. His eyes glowed a deep crimson-red, and his fangs were elongated. Blood dripped from his mouth and chin, and a loud hiss escaped his throat. But before he could make it fully from the room, Draven's quick draw already had him.

    With a single, fast shot to the head, Draven killed their old colleague.

Eleven

"What the hell just happened?" Zarah heard Nathanial shout from the end of the hallway as he approached them. When she turned her head, she could see he wasn't alone. Other Guardians were beginning to file out of their rooms, having awoken to the commotion, and followed him toward the medical area where Draven had killed Mitchell.

"Sir, Mitchell was Rogue," Draven began trying to explain, placing his gun back in the holster at his hip.

"That can't be. He came in clean. The staff checked him and didn't find any bite marks on his body." Nathanial argued with a low growl, now standing beside Zarah and Draven. His eyes darted down to Mitchell.

"It's true," Zarah interrupted, capturing Nathanial's attention once again. "The Rogues injected him with their poison or blood, instead of infecting him with a bite, so we couldn't see the small puncture wound of the needle."

Once Zarah said that, a few startled gasps went out through the crowd that had begun to surround them. Nathanial's eyes widened in horror as he shook his head in disbelief, and she looked grim. This was no joking matter.

Something happened then that shocked everyone.

Mitchell's body began to writhe. At their feet, it jerked and twisted while his eyes popped open and foam began to flow from his lips. The nurse that had been there earlier to help Draven hold the door against him screamed in revulsion, while the others began to back away in fear and surprise. Draven had shot him in the head; he should have died. A faint gurgling and muffled wail escaped from Mitchell while he continued to twist maniacally on the floor. His feet kicked at the linoleum. Something was horribly wrong.

Zarah yanked her pistol from her holster and fired. She couldn't stand to watch any longer. Firing three more rounds into Mitchell's head, he fell still at last and bled out. They knew then that he was really dead.

"What the hell was that?" Draven shouted, pointing at the corpse, and staring at Nathanial with wide eyes.

"That," Nathanial began, "was something I've never seen before. I think the Rogues are experimenting to even further advance themselves…and Mitchell might have been one of those experiments."

"It looks like we have an all-out war on our hands now," he added, looking up and making eye contact with both Zarah and Draven. The atmosphere in the Compound became heavy and tense. It was unnerving. They all became aware of the dangers they were now facing.

Zarah stalked away as a couple of Guardians stayed to help the nurse clean up the Hospital

Wing, and others crowded Nathanial to question him. She didn't notice Draven following her until she was away from the noise and in the comfort of one of the quiet hallways.

"I think I'd rather be alone right now, Draven," she said when she heard him behind her.

"Do you think the Rogues are trying to find a 'super gene'? Something like what you've got…maybe more than just a cure?" Draven asked, ignoring her request. She spun around so quickly that they nearly plowed into each other. Her eyes were fierce and angry.

"I'm not a freak, Draven. I don't know how I cured, or what they're doing. They're probably experimenting to build a higher race I'm guessing from what we just saw back there." She snapped. She was on edge.

"Now, goodnight."

With that, she turned and headed back into her room, slamming the door. Draven clenched his teeth in thought as he stood there for a moment longer before walking away to his room.

****

The next night, Zarah woke to thoughts still racing through her mind of the previous events. She couldn't shake the images of Mitchell. Fears welled up inside of her as questions rose through her mind. What kind of experiments would they perform on her if they captured her? Would she go through what Mitchell had because something was wrong with their formula?

With a low growl, she climbed out of bed and shook the thoughts away. No, they wouldn't capture her. She wouldn't let them. She would terminate herself before going Rogue again.

As she dressed, she began thinking of Thomas. If he was serious about helping them, she needed to inform him about what had happened with Mitchell. He had known him, too. Except she wasn't going to wait for Draven this time. She decided to go alone as she placed an extra gun in her holster at her waist, and a large silver dagger inside a black, leather strap wrapped around her thigh.

The hallway was empty when she stepped out and looked around cautiously. Secretly breathing a sigh of relief when she didn't see Draven waiting for her, she made her way out of the Compound and into the garage to begin heading to her brother's apartment. Zarah didn't have a car, and she wasn't about to be mean enough to steal Draven's, so she set out on foot, taking back alleyways through the city and keeping her senses on alert for any trouble.

The night air was warm and sticky, and a soft breeze carried many scents around her: flowers, wood, concrete, and coffee from a nearby late-night café. The moon was a thin sliver of eerie yellow and cast very little light as she strode along in the back alleys toward Thomas', but it didn't matter for her sensitive eyes. She still saw everything with great clarity. She kept her hand on the butt of her gun, ready to grab it at a moment's notice if needed.

Her walk was peaceful and quiet with the exception of her cell phone ringing once as she approached the apartment building where Thomas lived. Looking down at the screen, she saw it was Draven before she pocketed the phone again without answering. Some seconds later, it beeped to notify her of a voicemail message. She could only imagine him on the line, swearing, wondering where she had disappeared. It made her smirk in amusement.

"Zarah? What are you doing here? Alone, too? Are you okay?" Thomas started questioning her as soon as he opened the door and saw it was her.

"We need to talk," she said, pushing past him and into the apartment. Her hand was instinctively still on one of her guns, ready to pull it out and fire if needed at any second.

When she found that he had been alone in his place, she turned back and faced him quite a bit more relaxed.

"Where's Alyssa?"

"Out," he answered. He shut and locked his door before walking past her and taking a seat in one of the chairs in the living room. He motioned for her to have a seat across from him on the couch.

"What's going on?"

"Mitchell. He went Rogue. And not just Rogue...but something even stranger than that..." she began, taking a seat and then recounted every detail of what had happened the previous night. Thomas froze and went wide-eyed in shock as he listened.

"Mitchell was the tortured Guardian that you told me about being left in front of the Compound building?" he finally asked when she stopped speaking. Zarah nodded silently. Thinking back, she was relieved that whoever had left him still hadn't figured out how to get into their base at least.

"He had been a friend of mine at one time." Thomas whispered, turning his head away from her and looking out the window.

"I know," she replied. "It's why I came to tell you."

He turned back to her with a mischievous smirk and a glint in his red eyes.

"No, you're here for something else, too. I know you too well, little sister."

Before she could open her mouth to speak, there was a loud knock that quickly turned into persistent pounding, catching both of their attention. Thomas stood and crossed the room to open it. Zarah quickly reached out and grabbed his arm and motioned for him to be quiet as she slipped into a dark corner. Her gun was in hand in case it was another Rogue visiting her brother. He nodded at her, understanding her need to keep hidden and silently told her with his eyes that he would keep her secret. Seconds later, he unlocked the door and swung it open.

"I know she's here, damn it," Zarah heard Draven growl from the doorway.

Twelve

Zarah hesitated in the shadows of the corner where she stood, the gun still gripped in her hand. The tone of Draven's voice was enough to chill her. He was fuming, she knew, for leaving the confines of the Compound without him and going to Thomas'—a place that they shouldn't be trusting so easily yet to begin with.

"Maybe she's not," Thomas remarked, a sarcastic edge in his voice. She could hear the teasing smirk in his voice. She peeked around the corner with caution. This could end badly if she didn't step out soon. Draven's eyes glowed with rage as he took a step forward and withdrew his gun, directing it at Thomas.

"That's enough," Zarah said, stepping out

into the light and coming between the two.

"Put your damn gun back."

Thomas let out a low chuckle and shook his head in disbelief before stepping aside to let Draven into the apartment.

"You should really learn to trust me, Guardian, because I'm all you have right now as a source for information. Otherwise, you'd be blind, and then defeated, and my sister would be killed."

Zarah had already walked back into the sitting room, leaving the two guys at the front door. She hadn't noticed the way Draven stared over at her in concern after her brother's remark.

"That's what I figured." The Rogue muttered under his breath as the two entered the room. Only Draven had heard what he'd said.

"What are you doing here, Draven?" Zarah asked, finally looking over at him. She was seated on the couch again, her gun back in its holster, and she had relaxed by leaning back and propping her boots on the heavy glass coffee table in front of her, crossing her feet at the ankles. Thomas looked at her feet in annoyance. She raised her eyebrows at him and shrugged. He could clean his table later. He probably cleaned it ten times a night anyway.

"Looking for you, obviously," Draven answered, frustrated. Thomas took a seat in a black leather recliner across the room while Draven sat down on the other end of the couch with Zarah. His eyes remained on her, his lips pressed in a firm, stern line.

"You should have waited on me."

Thomas watched on in silent amusement.

"I don't answer to you, and I didn't have to wait," she turned and growled at him.

"It's apparent you had no trouble finding me, anyway.

"Zarah, it's too dangerous for you to be out walking alone!" He was in a near shout.

"I take care of myself just fine, thank you." She sat up straight, taking her feet off the table and glared at him. Thomas seemed to relax more when her feet came down. She refrained from making a sarcastic comment to him when his shoulders slumped in relief. Instead, her aggravation continued with Draven and she continued her argument.

"You, of all people, should know that."

"Up until recently, you didn't have Rogues hunting you down either," he remarked with raised eyebrows. His eyes shimmered in amusement.

"So? Bring them on." Her eyes narrowed.

"Damn it, you're stubborn."

"And you're an—" she started furiously.

"You know, you two argue like a married couple. This is quite a show," Thomas interrupted with a wide smile.

"Shut up!" The two turned and yelled at the same time. He only laughed and held his hands up in defeat. After his soft laughter died off, the room fell silent for a while with the exception of a nearby clock on the wall ticking away the seconds.

"In all seriousness, though, I do have to side

with him, Zarah. He's right. You shouldn't be out alone during this time. They are seeking you specifically to take to the Commander," her brother finally said with a sigh after a long pause. She glanced over at him and saw genuine concern...even within the depths of the red irises that marked him as one of *them*.

She gave a slight nod of defeat, lowering her gaze, but remained silent.

"How did you know she was here, anyway?" Thomas asked curiously, turning his attention to Draven.

"I know her well enough, I would have assumed her to have gone out hunting rather than here."

Zarah turned her eyes up sharply and clenched her teeth.

"Nathanial forced a Bonding Pact between us during my cure. I only just now found out about it recently," she answered before Draven could respond.

"Very interesting news. I never thought my

sister to settle down with a mate," he joked, chuckling.

"I am not settling down with a mate and it's not funny!"

"Relax, Zarah, I'm teasing."

She rolled her eyes and leaned back against the couch again, crossing her arms over her chest. Draven had decided to remain silent during the conversation, but now he stared at her with interest.

"What are you doing here, Zarah?" Draven asked.

She frowned and shook her head.

"I came to tell Thomas about Mitchell."

"No, not just that. As I said before, you're here for more, too," Thomas interjected, raising his eyebrows.

"I highly doubt the two of you are here to just hang out and watch movies all night."

Zarah sighed. "Alright, fine, I came to also ask a favor of you."

"Always with the favors…and yet, you're just going to kill me in the end when it's all over."

Her lips twitched in a smirk.
"Wouldn't have it any other way, brother."

"Well, maybe we won't," Draven cut in. "You have been helpful. If you continue to help us, maybe we could let you go when this is all over."

"We? There is no 'we', Guardian. You're lucky I let you slide when you put that gun in my face at the door," Thomas started with a growl, standing up from the chair.

"I will fight for my life against anyone else with the exception of Zarah. Only she can terminate me…and when she's ready, she can gladly put her gun to my temple and fire away."

Thomas' mood had grown dark, and Draven had pulled back at hearing those words. When he glanced at Zarah, he saw that she was staring at him in return, but there was a look in her eyes he didn't quite understand. Sorrow. Dark, deep, sorrow had filled her bi-colored turquoise-amethyst eyes and a moment of silence passed between the three of them.

"The cure. The Rogues are after Zarah for the cure, but what if we found it first?" Draven suddenly asked, finally managing to pull away from her gaze.

"I will not be a damn guinea pig," she argued as she shot down his idea.

"Can you do me the favor or not, Thomas?" She turned back to the subject she had started.

"I would never turn you down, you know that. What is it?" He crossed his arms. He was beginning to grow impatient she could tell. It didn't take her long to figure out then that Alyssa was out getting them 'dinner' and that he was probably growing thirsty. She quickly swallowed back her thoughts and concerns over whether or not they would still be there when her brother's mate would return with a human meal.

"We need someone on the inside so-to-speak for this Rogue Army. Think you can join it? You certainly have the credentials being an ex-Guardian," she finally stuttered out.

Thomas smiled.

"How do you think I've been getting some of my information lately? I'm an officer," he began.

The two Guardians stared at him in shock, waiting for him to continue with an explanation.

"The other night when you asked me to find out more information behind everything they're doing, that's the step I took for you, rather than just randomly questioning and having them get suspicious of me." He shrugged.

"And, Zarah, many of them live in this apartment complex... So, it's not very safe for you to be here," he added, concern crossing his features.

"We should go," she quickly said, standing as Draven followed. Just as she did, the bolt on the front door unlocked, capturing their attention, and causing the two Guardians to draw their guns in a flash.

Alyssa appeared in the doorway with a human male at her side. He seemed to be in a daze, unaware of the three other people in the front room. While she closed the door, she looked between each vampire nervously before meeting Thomas' gaze.

"I didn't realize we were going to have company," she said quietly.

"It's alright, sweetheart. Our Guardians were just leaving."

Zarah glanced over at her brother and nodded before she grabbed Draven by the arm and began to tug him toward the door.

"You mean we're just going to let them take the human?" he hissed in her ear.

"It's what they do. Besides, Thomas already said that he and Alyssa only take the bad ones," she replied quietly.

"Let him enjoy himself. I'm still killing him when this is all over, and he knows it."

"Goodnight!" she called over her shoulder as

they walked out of the apartment with a slam of the door.

When Draven and Zarah made it to the car, he stopped her before she could climb into the passenger side by touching her arm. She turned and looked at him in confusion. The night air had cooled some in their time at the apartment. Storm clouds were moving in, bringing in strong winds with them. The south always had strange, unpredictable weather. More so in the last two decades with many contributing global climate factors creating problems all over the world. Zarah loved autumn though, the season they were in right now. Nights were cooler, and the occasional storm was soothing.

"I want to know why you want to kill your brother. He is helping us. Don't you think that maybe we could help him in return?" he asked softly.

Zarah narrowed her eyes.
"He's Rogue, Draven. It's our job."

"And if there's a cure found?"
"No. I'm still killing him."

"So I think it's more than that. There's something you're not telling me. Tell me now. Why do you really want to kill Thomas?" he said, stepping closer to her. His voice was soft and he tried to reach out and touch her arm.

Her face grew dark as the wind continued to tumble around them. She turned without an answer and climbed in the car. She would not fall for the charm. He sighed and walked around to the other side to get in also. Zarah didn't want to tell him. They drove slowly in silence back to the Compound.

When they arrived, she tried to walk as quickly as she could to her room without any more conversation with him. There was no such luck. He caught up to her, grabbing her shoulder when she approached her bedroom door and spun her around to face him.

"I'm not letting this go. I want to know why it is you want to kill him. It isn't just because he's

Rogue." The charm he'd tried before was gone. Now it was serious.

"Damn it, Draven. It's not your business!" she started, her voice rising. It was becoming high-pitched and on the squeaky side.

"I want to know," he pressed. His volume was beginning to match hers. If they kept this up, they might draw some attention to themselves. "Why the hell do you want to destroy Thomas? And why is he so set on letting you as if he expects it?"

She opened her door and took a step inside before turning back to face him. He was taken aback by the sorrow and fury etched in her features.

"Really, I'm going to bed. Don't worry about it," she started, trying to soften her voice although her teeth were clenched. Her mind swirled and pleaded inwardly for him to go away. This was one of the many conversations she didn't want to have—a memory she wanted to lock away forever. She kept trying to push him away from her door. He was too tall. His hands held firm against her doorframe.

"No, I'm going to worry about it. Tell me." He'd reached the yelling point. She broke and dropped her hands, forgetting about trying to move him for a moment as tears sprung forward at the corners of her eyes.

"Thomas was the one that had turned me Rogue!" Zarah screamed back.

Zarah tried to slam the door in Draven's face.

"No, wait," he quickly said while shooting his hand out and stopping her again. "Stop doing that. Stop shutting me out every time you get angry. I'm tired of this door being slammed in my face."

She stared at him with narrowed eyes and shook her head.

"I have nothing else to say to you."

"Tell me what happened the night he turned you then." His voice had grown soft. When she met his gaze, she saw compassion and curiosity. His cerulean eyes shone intensely down on her, and his hands held steady on the open door.

Zarah remained silent, closing her eyes as

the memory and images flooded her from that night. All she wanted to do was forget, but it only haunted her now more than ever.

She had been chasing that bitch Rogue around on the rooftop of some abandoned building. After having finally shot the thing in the leg to bring her down, she got the job done with quickly in hopes to hurry and get back to the Compound before daylight.

But when she turned to go down the fire escape, there he was.

Thomas—her Rogue brother.

And what did she do? Absolutely nothing.

It had been six months since he had disappeared...since they had been ambushed that night and he had been bitten and dragged away by the rabid that still plagued her nightmares. Thomas looked the same with the exception of those burgundy eyes.

Those deep, crimson irises had stared

straight into Zarah's soul that night as he stood before her—and all she'd done was gaze back at him without making a single move. How many nights had she wandered the streets secretly hoping to run into her lost brother? She felt like she'd even allowed him to approach her, because when he did, she still didn't move. She had been frozen...stunned.

She snapped out of it though when he began speaking and tried to reach for her.

"Zarah..." he said, his voice barely audible.

Like the one who had stolen him from her, he spoke. Though he seemed to struggle with the words as if he was still learning, she'd heard him, and the confusion swept through her once again. It couldn't be possible.

Trying to reach for her gun, she fumbled, and he charged at her with his teeth bared. His voice chilled her. Her hands shook...and tears instantly stung at her eyes as she choked on a sob.

"You're not supposed to talk!" she screamed, still fumbling to grab her gun, dodging his attacks at the same time.

Their fighting was evenly matched. Where he was always the stronger one, she was always the faster one. She threw up a high kick to his jaw and knocked him back a few feet just as she managed to finally pull her gun free from the holster on her hip. Before she could fire, he was charging her again, knocking the gun from her grip and sending it flying across the roof.

He'd had her in his grip then, and no matter how hard she'd struggled, she couldn't break free...

"Little sister..." his tone was sinister in her ear. "Don't fight. You're only losing anyway."

When he bit into the tender flesh of her neck, a scream pierced through the cold night air. It only took a second for Zarah to realize that it was herself as her nails dug in and clawed at his back, and she continued to fight.

She remembered her scream slowly dying out as he continued to drink from her. She thought he was draining her dry rather than turning her Rogue until he released her moments later. When his grip loosened, she stumbled forward, landing on her hands and knees. He knelt down in front of her, taking her chin in his hand and turning her face up to meet his gaze. Their eyes met…and for a brief flash, she saw their father instead of him. Thomas looked so much like their father had…

Their parents. That was another story in itself. When they were young, still not fully fledged Vampires, their mother, a human, had been out shopping one evening when she had been attacked by a group of Rogues and ripped apart. As soon as their father found out, he went after the group on a mission of revenge, only to commit suicide by being turned Rogue himself. Three years later, Zarah and Thomas had to burn him one night. They promised each other that very night they would do what was necessary for the other if there was another situation like that. She was supposed to be Thomas' ticket to a release, but now how was that going to be possible if he'd just turned her too?

She had begun losing a lot of blood after that, but knew it wouldn't take long before the wound would heal as the rabid poison had already begun setting in. Her vision swam.

He stood, picking her up and carrying her

into the building where he sat her back down. He hadn't said another word since biting her, but she knew what he was doing. As she lay on the cold, concrete floor on her stomach, shivering and convulsing violently, Thomas had placed her there so she wouldn't be caught out in the sunlight. She had tried to crawl, to move and get out. What comprehension she'd had left told her to destroy herself before it was too late but the pain was too much, paralyzing her in place. Thomas cleaned her of all her weapons to be sure anyway, tossing them off of the roof.

"Thomas..." she stuttered out in a whisper, but he only started to walk away from her in silence.

"Thomas," her voice rose a little higher as she continued to watch his back retreating. Her lips were trembling then, her body frozen and paralyzed, and her head was spinning wildly as she tried to focus.

"Thomas! I'm going to kill you!" she finally screamed, hoarse. He stopped in the doorway, turning to face her....

And he smiled.

With that final image of him etched into her memory, he slammed the heavy, metal door, plunging her into darkness as she continued screaming for her brother. A few seconds later, she could no longer fight the pain or the spinning in her head, allowing her body to succumb to unconsciousness....

"Zarah?" Draven said, pulling her away from her thoughts and back to the present again. He was looking down at her with worry.

She swallowed the lump forming in her throat quickly, and regained her composure as she stood up straighter.

"There's not much to tell, Draven. He attacked me. He bit me. He left me. That is all." She tried to say it roughly but her voice cracked.

"Now, goodnight."

How could she be standing in front of him, acting so emotional, and expect him to care anyway?

As she started to close the door, he stopped her again.

"That's all? I hardly believe that is all there is to it..." he tried to argue.

Zarah narrowed her eyes and leaned forward. As she did so, she shoved his hand away from her door so that she would be able to close it.

"Thomas took a piece of my soul that night as he smiled and walked away. I don't think I can forgive that so easily," she said as she began to shut the door. Draven was left standing out in the hallway, stunned at her words.

Fourteen

Draven stood at Zarah's closed door. Leaning his forehead against the cool steel, he shut his eyes and took a deep breath. He could smell her on the other side; her scent was intoxicating as always. She smelled of a sweet mixture of fresh lilies, honeysuckle, and a hint of pineapple.

As thoughts began to race through his mind of how hurt she had looked when recounting her memories with Thomas and the night he had turned her Rogue, the fury started to build within him.

Draven opened his eyes and glanced down at his watch.

Three A. M.

He had plenty of time.

Listening at Zarah's door another moment longer, he heard that she was in the shower. Then, he pushed away and headed back toward the elevator to leave the Compound.

****

Zarah stepped out of the shower and walked into her room to grab sleeping clothes. That was when she noticed Draven had left from her door at last, and it made her let out a sigh of relief. The lump formed at the back of her throat was hard to swallow as her emotions ran rampant. His scent still lingered and she inhaled deeply, closing her eyes as she did. She couldn't allow herself to think, to get attached, like that. But, perhaps it was already too late.

"Such a fool," she chastised herself out loud with a shake of her head as she walked toward her little kitchen and grabbed a fresh bottle of blood. She was angry and embarrassed with herself for having opened up so much to Draven.

Draven…

Who had once annoyed and pissed her off so much…

Now, it seemed as if he genuinely cared. Even if he still liked to push her buttons to the boiling point. To top it off, she actually trusted him. More than anyone could even begin to imagine.

While she drank slowly from the amber-colored bottle, a small thought crossed her mind that nearly made her drop it.

It was possible she could be falling for him.

****

Driving, Draven looked around to see the streets mostly deserted at the late hour. It would have been peaceful if the anger in him hadn't been so much in control. He jerked the wheel to turn a corner, making the tires squeal. The radio blasted, heavy drums and blaring electric guitar riffs filling the space of the interior.

Zarah's voice edged into his thoughts.

"Thomas took a piece of my soul that night as he smiled and walked away."

He had remained silent throughout it all, and secretly had read her memories while she dredged them up. Draven knew she wouldn't tell the whole story...but he saw what exactly happened through her eyes as she stood there before him. There was something unusual there. Rogues were gaining intelligence long before he was aware of it, before this mission. Zarah knew it though. She had known the night Thomas was turned, and then again when he came back for her...

But it was that statement, the sorrow in her eyes, the pain in her voice, that'd struck him. When she closed the door in his face, he was floored beyond words. He didn't know how to comfort her.

He wanted to comfort her.

The rage grew as his drive came to an end and he slammed on his brakes, throwing the car into park violently. He climbed out of the car and stalked up to the door, and pounded on it.

After beating loudly, non-stop, for a few long seconds, the door in front of him finally opened.

"What?" Thomas asked in confusion, swinging the door open with a frown. He smirked when seeing Draven.

"Oh, Guardian, it's you," he began, looking around, frowning again at the odd situation.

"Is everything okay?"

Without a word and a sudden loud crack, Draven had brought his fist up and connected it against Thomas' jaw. It sent him flying backwards into the apartment, hitting a nearby bookshelf and landing hard onto the floor.

Thomas shot back up quickly, growling and baring his fangs. Draven, already inside the apartment, closed the door to the rest of the complex to keep the noise level down to a minimum as best as he could, but knew it wouldn't do any good if they were going to fight anyway. At that point, he didn't really care. His anger was winning out with his emotions, even if it was a little out of character for him.

The Rogue charged at the Guardian and slammed him against the wall. Draven swung again, trying to get another punch in, but missed when Thomas ducked. His hand went into a picture frame instead. Glass shattered onto the floor.

It was in that moment, Alyssa walked into the room from the back to see what the commotion was about and gasped, getting both of their attention.

"What is going on here?" she yelled at them.

"I don't know, ask him!" Thomas started shouting back.

"He's the one that came knocking, and then punched me when I opened the door."

Draven stopped fighting against Thomas and took a few steps back, clenching his teeth.

"What is your problem?" Thomas turned to ask Draven furiously, holding his jaw and shooing Alyssa's hands away when she rushed over to try and check on him.

"You did it. You attacked Zarah and turned her Rogue. You're her brother. Damn it, you're supposed to protect her, not ruin her." Draven's tone was ice.

Thomas raised an eyebrow, staring at him with interest. There wasn't any remorse in her brother's features, and that fueled his temper further. He began to ready his fist again and step toward him.

Holding up his hands up in defense, Thomas shook his head and pointed at the couch.

"Sit. There's probably more to the story you should know."

Draven froze and suddenly looked at him in confusion. More to the story? How could there be more to something like that?

Thomas glanced at him curiously as he sat in a chair.

"Trust me, Draven."

It was probably the first time the Rogue had addressed him by his name, and that was when he decided to sit and listen to whatever it was he had to say.

"I didn't want this. I knew she'd cure, and I knew it was only her that I'd want to end it for me. My sister wouldn't have unless I took extreme measures, so yes, I turned her Rogue," Thomas explained calmly.

"Do not think that I don't feel guilty about it. There's not a single day that goes by that I don't think of the pain I caused her. But, I know at the same time I protected her while causing my own end that should be done."

Draven inhaled sharply and looked at him in shock.

"You knew she'd cure? How?"

Thomas smiled then.

"A little family secret. Not even Zarah herself knows. It's rare, and if I tell you, you have to keep your mouth shut. Our father didn't want her knowing until the time was right, whenever I felt like it was good to tell her."

"Wait, wait. I'm confused now. Everyone has been trying to figure out how she's cured, but you're saying you've known all along?" Draven asked.

He frowned and shook his head, continuing his explanation.

"I wasn't there when she cured, remember? And I can't tell her right now. At this time, the main focus is to keep the Rogues away from the secret, and from getting to her blood for experimenting. It's to my understanding, they're already trying some unusual experiments."

"Yes, Mitchell was something unlike I've ever seen," Draven remarked as Thomas nodded thoughtfully.

A few minutes of awkward silence passed between them then as Thomas stared at Draven, lost in thought, concentrating and contemplating on what he was about to reveal to the Guardian. Finally, he sighed and uncrossed his legs.

"Unlike the lot of vampires, Zarah and I weren't born fully human or half-human first," he said at last.

"As I said, we are extremely rare cases,

probably the only two on the planet, and this is highly secret."

The normal life and turning of a vampire is that a male vampire can get a human woman pregnant, bearing a half-human, half-vampire child. The only vampire traits they show during childhood most times is faster-than-average-human speed, telepathy, burns from sunlight, and raw meat cravings. Then when the child reaches a certain age, usually the average around twenty, the father fully turns them by feeding him or her his blood. This stops the aging process, they never eat food again, and rely on the sustenance of blood to survive.

If a child is born to parents that are both human, and is thus a fully human child as well, the process is a bit different. Those vampires were turned later when they were older by another vampire in most cases because they became a part of the world, either through a mate, or because they were caught up in a fight. Some cases, like Draven, are a slight mystery. He woke up in a back alley late one night craving blood. Nathanial found him some hours later, and told him what he was. He had no memory of what had happened right before his turning, but he did remember small memories of his mother. Sometimes he missed her…but it had been decades, and there were a lot of blank spots.

"Okay, you have my attention." Draven sat up with interest.

"Our mother wasn't human. She was a Fallen Angel."

#

"What?" Draven stared in shock at Thomas, his eyes unbelievably wide.

"Are you being serious?"

"Do I look like I'm joking?" Thomas asked. He reached behind him and pulled a photo album from a nearby bookshelf. He reached across the table to hand it to Draven as Alyssa sat down in Thomas' lap.

There on the first page of the album was a family photo. Zarah must have been around the age of thirteen when the picture had been taken. Thomas was about sixteen or seventeen. They were still in their half-human states, not fully fledged. It was easy to tell by the markings on his and hers faces; they'd once had a sprinkle of freckles across their noses and cheeks. The change took them away later.

Behind them stood their parents and they were all dressed in rich, finely groomed clothes. Draven swallowed a hard lump forming in the back of his throat as his eyes landed on the woman that had to have been their mother. She looked human...but it was her eyes that held something strange in them. Her eyes were like Zarah's—a swirling mixture of two unusual colors. They were turquoise, almost the same bright shade as Zarah's, with swirls of intense gold. Her hair was short and black, but other features were certainly similar with Zarah: the full pouty lips, big doe eyes, and short, petite frame.

"How much has Zarah told you about our past?" Thomas split the silence, breaking through Draven's thoughts.

He pulled his gaze away from the photo and shook his head.

"Nothing, really. I struggled with her just to get a little information out about you and her going

Rogue. Even then, I had to search through her memories to get more to the story."

Thomas raised his eyebrows with interest.

"Okay, apparently it's true that she's fighting against herself from warming up to you," he joked. Draven frowned instead, and handed the album back after one last long look at the picture.

"What happened with your family?"

Thomas' eyes narrowed and he gently nudged Alyssa up from his lap.

"Sweetheart, can you leave us to talk alone for a while please?"

She nodded, leaning down and placing a soft kiss on his cheek, before walking out of the room. Draven watched her disappear into one of the back bedrooms until he turned his attention to Thomas again.

"Didn't she used to be a Guardian as well?" Draven asked with a frown. He thought he faintly remembered her. He had somewhat known Thomas from before, though not very well.

Thomas nodded as he stood and went to the kitchen across the room. He reached into the refrigerator and pulled out two bottles, holding one up to Draven as an offer. He looked a little hesitant, and it must have been clear in his face, because Thomas chuckled.

"It's safe. From the blood banks, I assure you."

"Alright, then," he said, and took a bottle from Thomas. As he swallowed down the rich, metallic flavors, he noted that Thomas could be trusted, and they sat down across from each other again. Thomas was hesitant to tell, but he started anyway, not meeting Draven's eyes. He stared out a nearby window as he spoke, distant, obviously getting lost in the memories.

"Our mother was a Fallen Angel. Our father was a vampire. That simple really, I guess. But she was so rare…such an unusual being. They agreed it would be best to just let everyone believe she was human and leave it at that. Very few knew her for what she really was. I only found out after her death."

"How'd she die?" The curiosity was building in Draven's core the more he was hearing. He even caught himself leaning forward with interest. His hands rested on his knees, fingers curling in eager fists.

"Zarah was sixteen, not fully turned yet, and I was twenty. My father was out hunting; he was a Guardian at the time. My mother had to go shopping. She could walk in sunlight during early morning hours when it wasn't too hot out, or early evening hours, but it was already after sunset. The store was only a five-minute walk away, and she was a fighter herself thanks to a lot of training from Dad. That night though, there were just too many rabids. She couldn't fight them all. They ripped her apart. I found her body. It'd been left on our front lawn. My father said that must've been where she was when they got her."

Silence stretched between Draven and Thomas. He had turned back to face him then, waiting.

"She was almost home. Right there in our yard, but we never heard her."

Draven could see the darkness in Thomas' eyes...the anger and sorrow over what had happened to his mother, his family, and he suddenly felt sympathetic.

"I'm sorry," was all he could stutter out.

Thomas waved a hand of dismissal. It was clear he wanted to quickly get rid of the images that still lived with him. His waving hand was probably not only shaking away Draven's sympathies, but the memory of his mother's mangled body splayed out on the damp morning grass.

"My father went crazy when he found out. He went on a suicide mission, leaving me and Zarah behind as he took off after the Rogues to hunt them down. He didn't know the exact monsters that'd done it, but he was determined to kill every rabid monster in a fifteen mile radius until he felt he'd had his revenge. Instead, it cost him his own life in the end. He was bitten and went rabid. Zarah and I had to hunt and kill him three years later after she was fully turned. We burned him inside our old family home," he continued.

"Were you fully turned at twenty then?" Draven asked.

Thomas nodded.

"Yes, luckily, my father had done that before he left on his damn mission to avenge my mother. Told me that if he didn't make it back, I had to be Zarah's protector, and that's what I've always done. I was the one that fully turned her when I felt she was of age and ready, the day after her nineteenth birthday. Yes, I also turned her Rogue, but that was because I knew it would protect her in the end."

"I still don't understand how you turning her Rogue protected her." Draven was still confused, the frown pulling down his mouth. He clenched his jaw to suppress the anger.

"As I told you, I knew she'd cure. After my mother's death, my father told me about her. There is a special gene that a Fallen Angel carries and passes onto their offspring that provides them protection from the poison. It's an immunity, so to speak. My father told me that it's only passed onto the females, so he was certain that Zarah had it. In order for it to take any kind of effect, she'd have to be turned Rogue first. The gene would then attack and kill the rabid cells over a short time until the cure is fully in place and the Vampire becomes normal again. After that, permanent immunity is in place and no matter how many bites she gets, Zarah can never be turned Rogue again," Thomas explained. He was getting annoyed having to talk so much, but had to admit that the Guardian wasn't so bad after all.

"It also activated the Fallen power. I'm not sure what yet, but something is different about her. Only time will tell, I guess," he added.

"So, what? Is she going through like a special growth? Developing over time? New emotions, special powers...that sort of thing?"

"I guess you could say that."

"What are Fallens exactly anyway? I'm not sure I understand that species. Where did they come from?" Draven continued to ask.

"Are we talking actual angels here?"

"You'll have to ask a Fallen that, which is difficult for us since they hate our kind. I couldn't explain it to you. I think that's almost like asking where we came from. Does one of us ever truly know the proper answer to that question? There are so many different legends and stories through history, it's hard to give one," Thomas explained.

He nodded in agreement. After another awkward silence, Draven's eyes grew wide as it all sank into place and he finally understood everything.

"But she wants to kill you now!" he suddenly yelled. Draven felt as if he had made a friend out of Thomas in the last hour and a half, even if he had entered by punching him.

"You need to tell her this, or she'll destroy you."

Thomas shrugged.

"That's just fine with me. I can't live like this forever."

****

Zarah was lying in her bed, watching boring reality television, when she smelled Draven coming down the hallway. His heavy boots echoed loudly on the tile, and she frowned.

Standing and running over to the door, she opened it, catching him just as he started to pass her door. He stopped when he saw her.

"Where were you?" she asked, eyeing him curiously.

For a few minutes, he remained silent and only stared at her intently as if he were lost in thought. Finally, he just smiled and shook his head, starting to walk away again as he answered.

"Nowhere. Don't worry about it."

"Mom is gone?" Zarah asked in a choked whisper, tears stinging at her eyes. She looked closely at Thomas, and suddenly narrowed her eyes when she noticed a difference. Gasping, she brought a hand to her mouth.

"You've been fully turned!"

He nodded and pulled her into a tight hug.

"Mom is gone. Dad has left. It's just us now, Zarah. I'm going to protect you, I promise."

Zarah woke the next evening and rolled over in her bed to stare blankly at her alarm clock. She let it blare with its annoying buzzing for a few seconds longer before reaching over to shut it off, letting her arm dangle lazily from the side of her bed afterward.

The dream had made her wake up. Anger and hurt consumed her as she remembered Thomas' words those decades ago…

"You broke your promise, big brother," she muttered out loud as she kicked out of her covers and stood to get dressed.

After she was ready, she heard a knock on her door. She knew it was him before she opened the door.

"Hey," she greeted casually. He smiled shyly and nodded in response.

Zarah grabbed her gun and holster, attaching it to her hip as she headed out of her room behind him. She had also placed a large knife in a leather pouch on the other side, and grabbed a shoulder holster and another small pistol hanging beside her lightweight, black knit duster jacket on a coat rack near the elevator.

"Did you make those?"

She was slipping on the black fingerless

gloves he'd been messing with on her counter a few evenings before. They matched her jacket perfectly. A brief nod was all she allowed before she stepped up to the elevator.

"Zarah," Draven began, sounding a bit soft-spoken and nervous.

"About last night... I'm really sorry I pushed you like that."

She held up a hand to stop him from saying another word.

"No, don't be sorry. It's fine. Sometimes I need to be pushed, I guess. You did have a right to know a little bit...and it was wrong of me to be so rude. It just...hurts...to talk about that stuff." Zarah looked down at her feet and shuffled them out of anxiousness.

"I understand," he replied.

She looked back up at him, meeting his eyes, and forced a smile.

"Zarah! Draven!" Nathanial's voice suddenly cut through the quiet hallway. They turned to see him coming at them with a big grin on his face.

"Come with me, please. I'd like to speak with you both in my office before you go out."

Zarah and Draven exchanged looks with each other, shrugging curiously, before following Nathanial to his office.

"What's going on?" Zarah asked once they sat down across from his desk.

Nathanial leaned back in his chair and placed his hands behind his head comfortably.

"I have a specific mission for the two of you tonight."

They remained silent, waiting for him to continue speaking. Zarah had a bad feeling creeping through her body that she couldn't shake. Almost as if her nerves were trying to warn her about something. Trying to shake the feeling away, she focused on Nathanial.

"The both of you are to bring back a Rogue captive for questioning."

Their jaws dropped and eyes widened at his command.

"What?" they both asked in unison, alarmed.

Nathanial frowned and leaned forward, placing his hands on the desk in front him in a firm grasp.

"You two will do as I say. Bring one back here. Alive. I want to question it. Now go."

They stood and left the office without argument. In silence, they headed to the elevator again and left The Compound. When they stepped out into the night air, they glanced at each other warily as they approached Draven's car.

"This isn't right, Draven." He revved the engine and put it into gear, reversing out of the parking spot, heading out of the garage and into the street with caution.

Draven stared straight ahead at the road lost in thought. Zarah was right. Something seemed a bit odd about it, but he wasn't going to question the motives of his boss. Maybe Nathanial had a plan behind this that would help them along in the end, and if they found a Rogue that was easy to question, they could get more answers. He glanced briefly at her to see her turned in the seat, staring at him with worry and silent questions. Those beautiful, big eyes glowed against the dash and it brought back the memory of his conversation with Thomas.

Half-Fallen, half-Vampire.

"Two halves…one known as 'good', one known as 'evil'. It's who she is. Always torn between the two. It's the result of the swirling colors in her eyes. Though we don't really know the true nature of Fallens really…but naturally, they're associated with the light side, while the vampire is associated with the dark."

"And what about you?" he had asked Thomas with a smirk. "You were born from the same mother."

"Yes, but I lost all of my light when I went Rogue. Hers cured her."

Zarah reached over and lightly touched his arm, getting his attention again.

"What?" he asked.

"I said, are you okay?" she said, looking concerned.

"You seem distracted."

He forced a smiled and nodded.
"Yeah, I'm fine. Let's just do what Nathanial asked. He apparently has some sort of plan that we aren't aware of."

She swallowed and nodded before leaning back against her seat and staring back out the window again.

****

"Zarah! Behind you!" Draven screamed.

Zarah quickly spun around in time to see a snarling Rogue flying at her. He had jumped from the roof of a low-lying nearby building in the back alley that they were standing in. They had been fighting another male Rogue, trying to subdue him enough to get him captured, when Draven had warned her of the incoming attack.

She was knocked backward into a brick wall, which stunned her momentarily before she regained her footing and began fighting. Throwing a hard punch, she connected with the Rogue's jaw first with her right fist, and then threw up her left leg to put a kick into his stomach. It sent him to the ground as he growled and screeched. Just as he was rising to come at her again, she yanked her pistol from her holster and fired a round into his shoulder, causing him to let out a howl of pain and grip his arm. The silver would certainly hold him back for a while; it wouldn't kill him until she struck a bullet into his head though.

    She made a quick glance back at Draven to see him still struggling with the other. Pointing her gun in that direction, she shot that Rogue in the leg once she was sure she had a clear shot. Draven looked at her in shock and relief. He had been fighting to hold a grip that he hadn't managed to get to his own gun. The Rogue in Draven's grasp fell to the street in pain, reaching for his leg with a yelp.

"Now the question is, which one do we take, and which one do we kill?" Zarah asked, looking at Draven. He shrugged, still holding the one by his shirt collar.

She looked at the Rogue that she had shot in the shoulder seeing that he was fighting against the poison and about to come at her again. His lips were pulled back, fangs bared, eyes glowing in rage.

Zarah took another glance at Draven with her eyebrows raised.

"Cuff the one you have, we'll take that one."

She turned in time as the other rabid prepared to jump at her again and fired a final shot into his head.

#

"Well, did you manage to capture one?" Nathanial asked when he looked up from his desk to see Zarah and Draven standing in the doorway of his office.

Zarah nodded solemnly.

"He's strapped down in a chair in an empty office. We also had the nurse inject him with a mild sedative when we arrived."

She thought about the drive back to the Compound. Draven had put the Rogue into the trunk of the car after tying up his legs and locking his hands together with silver cuffs. The gunshot wound in his leg had healed with the bullet intact, which was good for them because it meant the silver poison would remain in his system for a while. It didn't slow him down on the ride back, though.

The entire drive had been a bit noisy.

Kicking and muffled screaming had echoed through the trunk and into the interior of the car. Zarah kept turning her head to look at Draven in exasperation, who was obviously grinding his teeth and clenching the steering wheel as he sped back to the Compound. Tying up the Rogue's legs hadn't done much good really. He still managed to kick with his feet, and ended up denting the the trunk and busting out a tail light.

Needless to say, Zarah knew that Draven was in a bad mood after that ride.

"Alright then, let's go have a chat, shall we?" Nathanial grinned. He stood from his desk and grabbed a gun on his way out of the office. Zarah and Draven led the way to the room where the Rogue was being held. She kept her hand near her pistol, ready to take any necessary action.

When they all entered, they were faced with

the Rogue struggling to no avail against a number of silver chains and cuffs in a heavy, metal chair in front of a table. His eyes darted wildly around the room, taking in each Guardian, before landing on Zarah. His hair was long, black, tangled and shaggy. She felt nauseous as she eyed him over and saw a little dried blood crusted at the corner of his smirking mouth. When his dark red eyes wouldn't move from her, she shuddered and turned her head. Draven noticed and stepped protectively closer toward her, keeping a hand near his holster as well.

"What's your name?" Nathanial spoke to the Rogue, stepping forward. Zarah shut the door to the office but remained behind her boss and partner in the corner of the room.

He stared at Nathanial through narrowed eyes and snarled.

"Why in the hell should I say?"

When he snapped and began pulling at his chains again, causing the chair to scrape a bit on the floor, Nathanial walked over to him and grabbed him by the back of his hair. With intense speed, he slammed the rabid's face into the table. Zarah jumped as he shouted in pain and the metal echoed throughout the small space of the room.

Draven and Zarah exchanged brief glances of worry before turning their attention back to Nathanial and their captive. This was very unlike the behavior of the Guardians, and the two of them were a bit uncomfortable with the situation.

"Your name, Rogue. I'd like your name so that I can be a bit nicer and address you properly. Wouldn't you at least like that?" Nathanial growled near his ear, still gripping his hair.

"Jackson," he finally stuttered out in gasp. He inhaled sharply and tried to sit up straighter when Nathanial released him.

Nathanial grinned. Zarah swallowed back her fear and shrank back further in the corner. His grin seemed so...chilling.

"Well, here's the deal, Jackson. My two Guardians here have been trying to solve quite the unusual mission. You're going to tell us all you know. We may just let you live if you cooperate freely. If you don't, I can kill you," her boss said, continuing to smile as he loaded the gun in his hand before placing it on the end of the table in the Rogue's view for intimidation.

"I'm not saying a word. I don't know anything."

Before he could continue, Nathanial lashed out furiously with a roar and connected his fist with Jackson's jaw. The Rogue spat blood on the floor and turned back with a loud hiss.

Jackson looked vicious then.

"I think you will." Nathanial said calmly, pointing at the gun as a reminder of the deal.

After a few long minutes of being lost in thought, Jackson finally nodded.

"Only if you're serious about letting me go."

"Okay," Nathanial agreed with a smirk. "Zarah, Draven, go ahead and pull up some chairs."

She looked to see two chairs similar to what

Jackson was strapped in near the door. Quietly, following Nathanial's orders, she grabbed one and sat near the table, but still as far away as possible. Draven did the same, sitting near her. Nathanial grabbed a stool and sat closest to Jackson, looking highly amused by everything.

"So, Jackson, start telling us what you know," Nathanial commanded.

The Rogue looked cautiously around the room at them and his eyes landed on Zarah again.

"It's you. You're the one aren't you?" he suddenly spat out.

"What?" she asked with a frown.

"The one with the cure. We're all hunting you, you know. Some boss man we call 'The Commander' wants you. He says that he can create a cure if he just gets to you. The man is a genius. He's already made us intelligent obviously…that happened years ago. He refuses to tell us how he did that though," Jackson rambled. He talked fast.

Zarah narrowed her eyes but refused to respond, crossing her arms over her chest.

When he didn't receive a response, Jackson smirked and licked his lips.

"So, it is you…"

"Enough." Nathanial growled.
"Tell us about what happened with the Guardian that was left tortured and injected with rabid poison in front of the building here. His name was Mitchell."

"I had no part in that. I'm a loner!" Jackson yelled, suddenly frightened for his life. Zarah almost snorted out loud. He wasn't that much of a loner; he'd been fighting with another when they picked him up. She kept that to herself though. Apparently Draven wasn't going to say anything either.

Nathanial continued the questioning.
"What do you know though?"

"Some members of the Commander's Army ambushed him. The Commander has been creating experiments to make us more advanced creatures...some extra additions, I think. It's to my understanding they haven't exactly been working. The experiments have been dying off after a certain time period. They were very unusual. The Commander wants to create them to make us 'equal' or more superior to Guardians or something like that. If successful, your weapons would no longer be very effective in fighting us," the Rogue explained, sounding slightly confused. The silver was starting to control his system more, and it was beginning to exhaust him and slur his speech slightly.

"But from what I hear, all that stuff is just for show. For fun. Nothing The Commander is truly serious about yet anyway. His main focus is this girl," Jackson added.

"Hm," Nathanial said, thinking.

"Mitchell came back to life, well sort-of, after I shot him in the head. He had to be shot a few more times before he was fully terminated," Draven said as he joined the conversation. Jackson looked at him.

"Look, I'm being honest. I don't know much. All I know is that they want *her*," Jackson said with a snarl.

"In fact, she has quite the nickname among our kind. I don't know how it was picked up, but her body count may have something to do it."

"What would that be?" Zarah asked with interest.

"Angel of Death."

Draven froze and tried to keep his features emotionless. Surely the Rogues couldn't know her family secret? And if they did…that would mean that it was someone very close to her trying to harm her…

No. It had to be a coincidence. Just as Jackson stated, it had to have something to do with her famous Rogue body count.

Zarah snorted, oblivious to Draven's tensed up reaction next to her.

"Funny nickname," she muttered.

"Well," Nathanial started as he stood, taking the gun in hand. "If you have nothing else to offer us—"

Draven and Zarah jumped up together as Jackson looked at them all pleadingly.

"No! No! You said you would let me go free if I talked!" he started yelling, begging. Zarah had seen instances before where Rogues had pleaded for their lives, but this was a situation that she actually wished she could let this one go. They had captured and tortured him...it wasn't in their code. This was wrong, and the sinking feeling in her gut made her feel wretched.

"Ah, Jackson. I said that I would let you go. I didn't say anything about 'free'. I'm letting you go as a Rogue...meaning I'm releasing you of this life," Nathanial said with a mischievous smirk as he pointed the pistol at him. Jackson let out a choked sob. Zarah noticed how young he looked...he had to have only been around seventeen or eighteen when he was turned vampire, a bit unusual since most wait until they're twenty or older for the turning process. Perhaps he had been bitten as an innocent human to start with. Time seemed to slow as Nathanial's safety clicked off.

They shouldn't be doing this. She looked at Draven frantically.

It was as if he'd read her mind.
"Wait," he said.
"Let me do it. You probably have other work to do."

Nathanial stopped and looked at Draven. Jackson stared at him with begging red eyes.

"I have other things to tell," the Rogue quickly said in a desperate attempt to save his life.

"But I only want to tell them to those two...alone," he added, looking back at Nathanial.

Their boss looked at each one with narrowed, angry eyes.

"No, I believe we're done here."

The gun had a silencer attached so as to not raise any alarm inside the underground building. When Nathanial fired the round into Jackson's head, Zarah brought her hand up to her mouth to fight back a scream of protest and turned her head. It was the first time in her career that she must have felt remorse toward killing a Rogue. Nathanial set the gun back on the table when he was finished and smiled at them.

"I'll call the nurse to have her take care of the body. Good work tonight. Get some rest." He passed by them and left the room. Zarah was left standing there feeling the shock and horror weighing her chest down, unable to look toward Jackson's limp corpse.

Zarah stormed out of the office in fear of getting sick if she stayed in there any longer, and quickly walked toward her room.

"Zarah," Draven shouted at her from down the hall, trying to catch up with her. She stopped and waited, keeping her back facing him and her head hung down. Her weight was steadied against the wall as she leaned against it with her hands.

"Are you okay?" he asked when he reached her.

She slowly shook her head.

"It wasn't right, Draven. I respected Nathanial..."

She was whispering, confused and trying to fight back the oncoming tears.

"I don't care if Jackson was Rogue. That wasn't our way of doing things. It was just so...horrific...and he looked so young."

Draven sighed and looked around the empty hallway before speaking.

"I know. I tried to save him. I was going to let him go if Nathanial had let me take care of it. I don't think he was trying to be entirely cruel though. After all, he's still very angry after the Mitchell incident. Maybe that was his form of payback." Draven shrugged. When Zarah looked up into his eyes, however, she could still see him lost in thought, doubt lines etched around his down-turned lips, as if he still wasn't sure if his own explanation was convincing.

"Maybe you're right," she finally said with a sigh.

"Either way, I wish I hadn't been a part of that."

He pulled her into a tight hug at that moment, which surprised her.

"Me, too," he said.

Her phone rang a second later, making her pull away from him awkwardly to answer.

"Hello?"

"Hey, sis."

"Thomas. Hi," she replied. She looked at Draven to see him eyeing her in confusion.

"What's going on now?"

"I'm afraid I have some unsettling news to give you. I just got back from a meeting," he began.

She paused and listened intently. It was after a few seconds that she realized she'd been holding her breath.

"The Commander is moving on to bigger things. He's decided that once he's extracted the cure from you, he's going to start harvesting humans and out the vampire race. Which of course could result in a very nasty war as you know."

"What?" Zarah nearly screamed.

Eighteen

The next evening Zarah was lacing up her boots, ready to go out hunting again, when Draven arrived.

"Come in," she called out as she crossed her room and entered her kitchen to grab a bottle of blood to drink before leaving. He opened the door and stepped inside as she popped the lid off and began gulping it down.

"Want one?" She took a deep breath when she finished with her first long drink.

He shook his head but forced a smile. "No, thank you."

"Have you heard anything else from Thomas?" he added, taking a seat at the barstool near the counter.

"No, not since last night," she replied with a frown. She finished the rest of her bottle and then rinsed it out in the sink. Draven was across the room looking down at her pile of arts and crafts. He glanced back up at her with an unusual expression. She realized he was holding in a laugh.

"What?"

"Cross-stitching? Seriously?" He held up a cute picture of a kitten that she'd been working on recently. The thread still hung loose in some areas on the plastic backing, and the tail of the orange kitty wasn't complete. She ran forward and grabbed it from him.

"Shut up! It's entertaining."

He snorted and she stuck her tongue out at him, which only caused him to laugh harder. Tossing it back down among the other things, she shook her head with a playful smile.

"Let's go."

Thomas hadn't had much information to give them when he called, only what was learned at the meeting he'd attended the previous night. The Commander was out for a major world war between humans and vampires, and had every intention of turning the planet to Hell basically. That was all they knew. Zarah and Draven had talked before parting for bed...they would have to find and destroy the Commander very soon—before he found her or before he started putting any of his plans into effect. Tonight, they were going to start hunting down some of his army members. They were going to have to toss out their 'code' and restrain some of the Rogues in order to question them as well.

They weren't entirely thrilled with their plans of what had to be done, but they knew it was the only way of finding the Commander's whereabouts. Thomas didn't know. He'd told them that some of the older members probably would. So, he gave them an area that he knew the two Guardians would find them.

He'd overheard many nights that was where they liked to "play" around in the city the most due to more humans trafficking through the area.

As Zarah finished attaching her abundance of weaponry to her body, Draven stood idly by at the bar and watched. When she noticed his gaze, she raised an eyebrow.

"Hmm?" she asked.
"Nothing," he replied with a shrug, continuing to stare.

She sighed as she placed extra gun clips on the inside pockets of her jacket.
"If you have something to say, just say it."
"Just…be careful out there, okay?" he finally said after a long silence, crossing his arms over his chest.
She looked up at him with a smirk.
"I always am. The same goes for you, too, though."

With the brief words exchanged, they headed out of her room. Draven slipped his jacket on in the hallway as the two of them walked toward the elevator. Nathanial was waiting for them there, still unaware of their plans and how they had been having Thomas as a source. He smiled as they approached.

"I expect another Rogue brought to me later tonight," he began.

"I likely won't be here when you return. I have somewhere to go, and many of the others are going out on their own rounds tonight as well, but I trust that you two will be able to handle yourselves well enough. Detain it in the same room as the other one had been in."

Zarah glanced at Draven, maintaining a straight face. Lately, she'd begun really disliking some of her duties. It had nothing to do with her partner anymore, but with how things had changed within the Compound. Taking Rogues for torture tactics until killing them…that was not their way of doing things. That had not been how she had been trained. Maybe they deserved it for things they had done, but the Guardians were known amongst the vampire community for having good, high-standing morals and respect. A lot of Rogues were killed quickly, without the torture, because that was seen as a sign of respect toward the fallen, corrupted vampires.

Draven nodded at Nathanial and checked to make sure the safety of his gun was on before replacing it back in the holster at his waist.

"Sure, boss," he muttered, avoiding eye contact with anyone.

Zarah felt the anger flare up within her chest. She knew he hated it just as much as she did.

"Nathanial, we don't like this," she turned and spat out with a frown.

"What the hell is wrong with you?"

Draven looked at her in shock.

Nathanial narrowed his eyes and stepped closer toward her. His approach was menacing but she held her ground and kept her head high, continuing to stare at her mentor with her jaw clenched tightly.

"What's wrong with me is that I'm done playing games amongst our kind. Rogues,

Guardians, Hiders…we're all Vampires. Some are corrupted and need to be killed. Some should rule the world," he began with a growl. Gaining his composure a second later when she remained silent, he smiled at her.

"Of course, that would never happen though. Vampires trying to rule the world. That's just ludicrous. This is the humans' world. Not ours. We are mere shadows in the dark to them."

She blinked at him.

"Things have become even more out of hand than what most of us are capable of handling, I think, with the exception of you two. This is war, Zarah. And I intend to do whatever it takes to put things to an end. Have a good night."

With that said, Nathanial stepped around Zarah and continued on down the hallway into his office, leaving the two of them alone at the elevator.

She turned to look at Draven in confusion.

"Did you tell him anything about our secret mission?" she asked, barely above a whisper. Concern was clear in her features. Nathanial's reaction had been a bit strange for her…almost insane.

Draven shook his head and frowned.

"No, but that was an odd conversation. Even for him."

She nodded in response and hit the elevator button as she got lost in thought.

The more she began to think about it, the more she realized that through the years she had never paid too much attention until that moment that Nathanial had always been one of the rare supporters of the vampire race living openly amongst the humans. He always said it would be more peaceful that way, and that they would likely get a larger Guardian base. In a way, she saw his point. However, she didn't agree with a world war to dominate the humans. Nathanial was her mentor. Her life-saver. He agreed with her on that, too.

"I'm pretty sure he meant nothing by it," she finally said as they stepped into the elevator.

"He gets in some strange moods sometimes.

Especially when he's passionate about something."

"Like when it comes to Rogue hunting?" Draven joked, laughing. She let out a soft chuckle and nodded while they were brought up to the parking garage.

****

Their night was not going well.

Two Rogues had already escaped from their sight, managing to lose the Guardians by disappearing through winding back alleyways. Zarah was getting frustrated.

Draven drove toward the heart of downtown and pulled the car into an abandoned lot. When they parked, he looked over at Zarah with a forced smile.

"Let's just take it fully on foot from here. This is the area," he said. She nodded and stepped out of the car with him.

Looking around, she noticed they were at an area known as "the crossroads." It was the exact center of the city where there was one main intersection with four roads that then began branching out to the rest of the countless streets and other highways. The Crossroads was the area that Thomas had recommended they looked around, due to the number of buildings and parks surrounding the corners. Reaching under her jacket, she retrieved her gun from her holster and kept her senses on alert.

As if on cue, one Rogue strolled by across the street from them, heading toward an empty building. He stopped in his steps when he sensed the Guardians and turned to face them with wide eyes. Zarah smiled mischievously and glanced at Draven, who was already by her side with his gun drawn as well.

"Ready?"

"Yep." She took the safety off her gun.

They ran forward together as the Rogue started to run away from them and toward the empty building.

Zarah fired her gun, but missed, and cursed under her breath.

The Rogue ran into the building before either Guardian could get in another shot. Draven continued on with the chase and sprinted toward the doorway. There wasn't a door, only a frame, and darkness seeping through from there. The wood was worn, paint peeling, and windows were mostly broken or dusted over. It was large, and there was something ominous about the feeling in the pit of Zarah's stomach. Déjà vu struck her in waves…but Draven had already entered, and she was still standing outside, her feet frozen in horror.

"Draven! Wait!" she quickly shouted, running in as worry sunk into her bones.

Her eyes adjusted to the darkness abruptly. It was much darker within the building than outside, but she could still see. Small beams of moonlight leaked through the broken windows and cast a soft, silver glow in some areas. Inside, it was a mess of glass, shredded papers, and rubble.

The Rogue was nowhere in sight.

She stood closely by Draven, the both of them looking around for any kind of sign of movement.

When she heard some rubble get moved across the room from being kicked, Zarah fired her gun in that direction.

Some seconds later, chuckles, snarls and hisses could be heard from all around them. The hideous sounds of the corrupted vampires echoed through their ears, sending chills down to their bones.

Zarah slowly turned her head left and right, looking in each direction, to see the bright glowing crimson eyes of about ten Rogues that surrounded them then in the corners and along the sides of the room. They had been well hidden to them when they first entered.

"Draven," she began barely above a whisper, stepping closer toward him as they both gripped their weapons tighter.

"Yeah?" He looked around to see what she was beginning to see as well.

She locked her eyes on his and they widened in fear.

"We've been ambushed."

#

The rabids attacked first.

Draven grabbed Zarah and pulled her closer against him as they began firing their guns at the oncoming beasts. Snarls and laughter ripped through the silent night air and echoed off the abandoned concrete walls of the old factory building the two were trapped in.
They continued firing rounds in all directions around them until their guns clicked. Empty.

The Rogues were still coming at them even as Zarah loaded her last clip into her pistol. She had managed to throw a hard punch to one in the jaw as it had come too close to them before she could fire a shot, giving Draven enough time to reload.

Relief flooded her when she noticed their numbers dropping. She spun around and kicked a Rogue in the gut that sent him flying into a nearby wall and rubble crashing down from the impact.

When she turned back, she saw Draven smiling at her and not another rabid creature running at them to attack. Finally able to take a deep breath, she smiled in return.

Her grin faded, however, when low growls began to rumble throughout the building causing her to spin back around in alarm. Her hair flew around her face in a rush of dark copper; her eyes were chaotic and frenzied. Draven reached out and grabbed her arm.

"There's more," he whispered. Zarah didn't need to be told, she could already see the formation of the Rogues surrounding them. Their red eyes were glowing with menace and hunger set against the smoky abandoned room they had been led into.

A rock from nearby was kicked into her boot and she turned sharply in the direction of the door where it had come from with her gun aimed, prepared to fire. Instead she locked eyes with Thomas, who had his hands quickly raised in defense. Alyssa stood next to him, looking ready for a fight as she held her own pair of pistols as well.

"Thomas," Zarah barely breathed out just before the attacks began from the Rogues behind them.

As the fight ensued, the numbers overwhelmed them. The two Guardians and their two Rogue allies fought hard against the attacking monsters. They spread apart to fight larger numbers—Zarah fighting near Thomas, and Draven fighting across the warehouse near Alyssa.

"What are you doing here, Thomas?" Zarah asked her brother with a frown, shooting a Rogue in the head as he ran at her with his fangs bared. She was running low on ammo and would soon need to start fighting hand-to-hand with her silver knives. It was combat that she was skilled in, but not particular fond of when they were so outnumbered.

"I came to help, of course," he replied with almost a laughing shout. "I heard what was going on from some sources and I knew I couldn't leave you to fight this alone."

For the first time in years, she was fighting alongside her brother again. Every few seconds, she'd check out of the corner of her eye and almost smile while watching his fluid, graceful kicks at the oncoming attacks. His weapons had run out of ammunition shortly after hers. The four of them were all fighting with just their silver daggers then, and the numbers only seemed to keep increasing.

Zarah tried to look for Draven, but couldn't keep him in her line of vision anymore. The crowd was too large and blocked her view from where he was fighting at across the warehouse.

"Thomas, this is too much! We have to get out of here!" Zarah shouted as she sent a female flying through a nearby window. The glass shattered and sent shards upon two Rogues below. One let out a wail that pierced her ears.

When the two monsters began to advance on her again, she saw the pieces of glass embedded in their faces and arms. Thomas ran up beside her. One Rogue that approached had a large chunk of amber glass protruding from his eye and blood running down his cheek. Their snarls were feral. The Rogues that ambushed them were not the new intelligent breed that had been developing. But as she looked around, Zarah felt a strange disturbance and her brows furrowed in thought. They had to have some intelligence if they had ambushed the Guardians. Or were these Rogues under some sort of mind control?

"I have a way to get us out," Thomas whispered near her as the Rogues continued advancing.

She looked at him, and then briefly down to his hand where she saw a small black tube. He had an explosive. Not just any explosive, either. A rare one that Guardians used to possess, but no longer use due to development issues. Mostly the issues were that Thomas had been the Guardian that created them in the first place. He knew the formula. When he went Rogue and left, that formula and the weapon left with him.

Zarah didn't have time to question him. A small piece of her felt grateful he was on their side, and even though he was corrupted by the rabid poisons, he fought hard against them. He proved it very simply just by showing up. She nodded quickly and they turned back to their attackers.

The first one, the one with the glass embedded into his eye, lunged at her. She blocked him quickly with a swift punch to his throat. As he staggered back, gasping for a breath, the other Rogue took aim at Thomas. She couldn't watch the two scuffle though. She had to remain focused on the one in front of her, who was already preparing to attack again. In the meantime, more were beginning to descend upon them, to outnumber her and Thomas. Zarah had her silver dagger in hand and was slashing at whatever she could.

Thoughts of Draven drifted into her mind as she fought her way through the numbers furiously. Where was he? Was he hurt? She couldn't see him, and it began to set her nerves on edge. There were so many of them. What if he had been bit? Her partner couldn't lose his life that way and there was absolutely no way Zarah would bring herself to kill him if it came to that. Draven and she never got along before, but this mission had changed something between them drastically. He was now something she'd call a…friend. Something clicked, though, that sent a flood of relief through her. Draven couldn't be hurt. He was alright. He was there somewhere amongst the fight, unable to be seen, but she knew he had to be fine. She remembered the Bonding Pact. If something happened, she'd know on instinct through that connection.

Distractions of her thoughts threw her off balance. Glass Eye, as she had already nicknamed the Rogue, grabbed her from behind and slammed her against a nearby wall. The force of the impact caused her to drop her knife.

As Zarah struggled against Glass Eye, he hovered above her. His fangs glinted against moonlight, dripping with blood and saliva, and his breath was raspy and foul. She feared the worst. She was going to get turned Rogue again. And if she did, would she be so lucky to cure a second time?

He was strong. It was a trait that any Rogue would have. More strength due to the powerful bloodlust they were lost to. She couldn't move much under his intense grip as he held her arms pinned above her head against the stone wall. Her legs tried to kick at him, only to slip on the rubble beneath her feet. Glass Eye was smiling something nasty and headed right for her throat.

Then things began to happen in a flash.

When Zarah thought she was going to lose her life again, Glass Eye pulled back with a screech and blood splattered out onto her face. His grip released and she looked up to see a metal rod protruding from his chest, Draven standing behind him with a smug smile. He was still holding the rod behind the Rogue.

"Let's have some fun."

Zarah pushed away from the wall and shook her head at Draven's remark, picking her knife up from the ground. She looked around, seeing Thomas and Alyssa fighting together nearby. The number of Rogues were finally dwindling. The battle was becoming easier, but she could tell that they were all beginning to tire out. The sun was going to be up soon, too.

With still-shaky hands, she brought her knife up to Glass Eye taking one last look at him. So close he had come to getting her. He was struggling against the rod, trying to remove it with no luck. He curled up his lip with a growl as she approached him. Furiously, she bared her fangs and glared at him in his good eye.

"You lose."

At that, she took her blade and dug it deep into his heart. When Draven let his body fall, it slumped against the same wall that he'd held her against. The silver poison worked quickly and within a matter of seconds, the rabid was only an empty shell. His one red eye stared blankly up at the ceiling, and his mouth went slack.

She turned back to Draven.
"Come on, we have to get out of here. Thomas has—"
But before she could finish her sentence, another Rogue had descended upon them, this time coming up on Draven behind his back. Zarah froze. Something flashed in the Rogue's hand. She regained her senses and tried to move forward.

"Draven, look out!"

It was too late.

By the time he turned around to try and deflect the oncoming attack, and she was running forward to try and help, the Rogue plunged a silver knife into Draven's side. Zarah stood still, shock consuming her as he let out a cry of pain and fell to the dusty floor. The seconds that ticked by seemed to move in slow motion. All at once, emotions overpowered her and she began to lose her senses.

"No!"

She screamed so loud, it was deafening, and drowned out the fight around her. The Rogue looked from Draven to her, cocking his head to the side. It was mocking and it only made the rage bubbling within her grow. Something snapped and she began slow steps toward the creature, gritting her teeth. The white-hot sensation at the pit of her stomach returned with a frenzy. The violet pulses flashed in her peripheral again.

Draven was clutching his side after tearing the silver blade from his body, the blood pooling down his hands. His hands were shaking and he remained on the floor, in too much pain from the slow-moving silver poison in his veins to move. He hadn't been stabbed through the heart, so he could live if he made it back to The Compound in time to receive care. If they could all get out of this fight. Zarah glanced at him to see how badly injured he was. He needed help fast.

She stalked up to the Rogue, only fueled by the growing heat in her own core, and before he could react, lashed out. Her hand found a tight grip around his throat and with rage-induced strength, lifted him from the ground before slamming his back against a wall to pin him there. This time, it was she who cocked her head at him in a mocking manner and then smirked. The Rogue gasped for breath and his eyes widened in terror as he tried to struggle against her grip, to no avail.

"You stabbed my partner." Her voice was haunting, low and menacing.

Another creature tried to attack her from behind, but her senses were on such high alert, she didn't even flinch or lose her grip. She simply used her one free hand, and stabbed the other in the heart in a blinding, angry flash with her silver blade, watching only for a second as he staggered away a few feet, and then collapsed among other bodies to die. When she turned back to the struggling Rogue again, her smile was deadly.

"Zarah…"

When she heard Draven, she whipped her head around and looked down. His eyes were wide, in awe of something she was unaware of, and he was still clutching at the wound in his side. She could tell he was in a good deal of pain. Looking around, she suddenly noticed the fighting had ended, and everyone was staring at her, either in awe, or in pure terror. The Rogues were backing away, a lot of them starting to run out and disappear. Thomas was almost smiling.

"What?" she asked with a frown.

About that time, she heard an odd sizzling

sound beneath her fingertips and smelled burning flesh. The Rogue that she held started screaming and writhing, fighting to get loose. She turned back with wide eyes, seeing that her hands were burning the creature. Unable to let go at first from shock, the burning became more intense, going deep through the neck as tissue and muscle began to char. Smoke billowed from the rabid's screeching mouth. When flames erupted, she dropped him and jumped back, staring at her hands in confusion.

"You're glowing," Draven finally said, finishing his thought from a few minutes before. She looked back up, her jaw dropped open in shock and then her partner fell into unconsciousness.

It was starting to fade, her normal pale-white skin tone returning, but when she stared down at her hands, she saw briefly that indeed she had been glowing—a very soft violet emitted from her body and lit the dark room around them. Whatever it was that had happened, it had made her kill with just her bare hands.

Twenty

Zarah rushed over to Draven, trying to forget the incident. Her only concern in that moment was him. The silver poison was taking over and it showed through his skin. Lines of gray had begun to run along his arms, and his breathing was labored. She knelt beside him and began fishing through his pockets.

"What are you doing?" Thomas asked as he walked over.

"Looking for his keys. We have to get out of here."

When she found them, she stood and faced her brother. Behind him, the Rogues that remained in the warehouse were already starting to get brave again, preparing to advance. There weren't many left, and they stayed close to the back corners, their growling echoing off the concrete walls. Some curses were hissed and Zarah distinctly heard "Angel of Death" from a few whispering, raspy voices. Her nerves were set on edge.

Without any question, Thomas leaned down and picked up Draven, hoisting him over his shoulder with a grunt.

"Damn, Guardian is heavy," he breathed, and they started running for the door.

As they reached the front entrance, Thomas reached into his front pocket with his free hand and thrust the black tube at Zarah. She knew how to set it off, and that's what he wanted her to do while he carried Draven and led Alyssa toward the car. She nodded and watched them continue to run on as she remained standing in the doorframe, staring at the cluster of Rogues across the way.

They were preparing to charge toward her; she was faster. Snapping the trigger at the top of the tube, a loud buzzing began to sound off and a blue light blinked at the bottom. The Rogues stopped and stared curiously at the weapon in her hand.

"Head's up!" she shouted, tossing it into the warehouse. The metal clanked and it bounced and rolled a few feet before coming to a stop shortly in front of them in the middle of the room. The buzzing became higher pitched. They started to back away, scrambling to get out through the back, as she took off running toward the car with a slight limp in her left leg from the earlier scuffle with Glass Eye.

The explosion hit before she could get to the end of the sidewalk. It blew her forward, sending her sprawling on the concrete with a scream and ringing in her ears. Through the noise, the shrieks and anguished cries of the dying Rogues filled the night air.

Zarah turned slowly and looked back at the building. It was bathed in blue flames. Inside, she knew the remaining rabids were covered in tiny embedded silver pieces. The poison and chemical fire would kill them soon enough. If not, it would paralyze them until the dawn, and the morning sun could burn them to ash. It was the rare weapon that her brother had created—the weapon he had just used to save them with. She had been blown forward on the sidewalk by the wind of the blast, but was luckily unharmed other than a few serious bruises and scrapes.

Zarah stood and continued limping onto the car as the Rogues still screamed inside.

****

The car beeped as she hit the remote button to unlock it when she approached.

"Put him in the passenger seat."

"Zarah. You're hurt," Thomas said as she opened the car door and he placed Draven in, buckling him in.

"I'll be fine. You and Alyssa need to go. That blast is probably going to attract human attention soon." She looked down at Draven. He was still unconscious. Closing the door, she started toward the driver's side with the key in hand. To hell with never being allowed to drive his car, this was an emergency. She'd deal with his attitude later when he was healed.

Thomas and Alyssa had already started walking away with their hands tightly wound into each other's. Zarah stood at the car for a moment watching their retreating backs.

"Thomas."

He turned back and faced her. When she met his red eyes, she had to stop from recoiling, her instinct…her memories of what had happened between them… and fight back the constant nagging grudge. That night, he had been her brother again. Her face softened and tears nearly stung her eyes.

"Thank you."

Thomas nodded, then waved her off. Zarah had to hurry and get Draven to The Compound. She had so many questions to ask, especially about what had happened with her back in the warehouse, but the questions would have to wait.

She quickly climbed into the car, revving the engine and sped toward The Compound as fast as Draven's car would go—tires squealing around every corner she took.

When she turned into the parking garage, Draven groaned, coming back into consciousness. Zarah could tell he was in a lot of pain and looked at him warily out of the corner of her eye. Slamming on the brakes as she put the car in park, she turned and unbuckled him.

His eyes were gazing at hers, half open and he was wincing where he clutched at the wound.

"I thought I said you could never drive my car."

"Well, I think this situation could be an exception," she whispered back, meeting him with a smirk. He swallowed against the pain and nodded slowly before closing his eyes again. Sighing, she climbed out of the car and left him, running into The Compound to seek help from the medical ward because she knew she wouldn't be able to carry him in.

The hallways were empty as she ran around the corners. Looking down at her watch, she frowned. The others should be starting to come in from their own rounds about then, or at least very soon. She found it strange that The Compound was so completely empty feeling. Normally, at least one or two Guardians may take the night off to stay behind and keep watch there.

"Hello!" Zarah pounded on the metal door that led to the infirmary.

"I need your help out here. Open up!" Her throat ached from all the shouting she had done in the last few hours, her voice already beginning to grow hoarse.

When the door swung open, a bewildered nurse stood before her. Rarely ever did the

Guardians need the medical wing, except on serious occasions such as with Mitchell, the Guardian who went mutant Rogue. The nurse that stood in front of her then was the same one that had assisted them that same night. She looked taken aback by Zarah's disheveled appearance.

"Zarah! Are you okay? You're hurt! Get in here and—" she started in a rush, reaching out.

"No! Not me, don't worry about me. I'm fine. It's Draven. Come on, and bring a chair. He's critical." Zarah bent over trying to catch her breath. "Is there anyone else here that can help? Where's Nathanial?"

The nurse, Cathy, was already wheeling a chair out into the hallway with a shake of her head.

"They're still all out and haven't made it back in from their rounds yet. Nathanial went out, too. Just us now."

Zarah nodded and they began racing back toward the car again to get Draven. Between the two of them, they should be able to get him into the wheelchair and down to the medical ward. There wasn't a doctor anymore since Mitchell had killed the other, but Cathy was perfectly capable of handling the situation.

"Oh my… Zarah… What the hell happened to you two?" she slowly asked when seeing Draven.

"We were ambushed by a very large pack of Rogues in an abandoned warehouse."

"You're lucky to be alive. Two against so many," Cathy replied. They carefully pulled him out of the seat, and with a little struggling, finally managed to get him in the wheelchair with a white blanket over his lap.

Zarah stared down at him in silence, watching the blood stain already beginning to form through the sheet. He groaned in pain as he went in and out of consciousness and they started quickly back toward medical.

"Yes. Lucky," she barely whispered. Zarah knew it wasn't just luck, though.

****

She felt odd sitting in the waiting room while Cathy was in the examination area tending to Draven. The seconds on the wall clock above her seemed to tick loudly against her temples as she tapped her foot to a rhythm. Her limp from earlier was already starting to feel better. Zarah had always been a fast healer.

"Zarah?"

She looked up to see Cathy standing near with a solemn expression.

"I have good news, and I have bad news."

Zarah stood, taking a deep breath. Looking quickly at the clock again, she saw that barely fifteen minutes had passed since Draven had been taken into the examination room. That had been some speedy service. Or was that part of the bad news? Was something so terribly wrong and unable to be fixed that there was nothing more Cathy could do? Where the hell was everybody else and why were they so late coming in from their rounds, anyway? She frowned and turned back to the nurse with a nod.

"I can take it, I think."

"Draven's wound has been stitched up, though, it won't take long for him to heal—a matter of two days at most—so the stitches will just dissolve as he heals," Cathy started.

"Okay...and? What's the bad news?"

"He needs blood."

"So? Give him some. There's plenty of it bottled around here," she frowned.

"If that's the bad news, then you have to do better than that to set my nerves on edge, lady, because I just faced about sixty or more Rogues back there. And more kept coming in."

"Not that kind of blood, Zarah." Cathy stopped her, gripping her arm and pulling her back toward the examination room.

Zarah had been about to walk out once she was sure Draven was alright, ready to go to her room, and collapse from exhaustion. Upon hearing what the nurse just told her, she froze and stared wide-eyed at her.

"Wait, what?"

"A Vampire's blood. He needs it. Soon. Or he will die," Cathy explained, enunciating slowly.

"Then give him yours! I can't do that!"

"No, I can't. I'm on duty, Zarah. It's not permitted. You have to do it. You're here now. And there's no one else to do it."

"You don't understand. He won't take from me. I'm tainted. That's what he said. I believe him, too. It's not safe. I can't let him feed from me." Zarah was rushing her words, panic rising in her chest. The nurse began dragging her to the examination room.

"Well, you have to try."

Before further protest, she was shoved in the room with the door closed behind her.

Twenty-One

Draven was laying in front of her. The room was very small, and suddenly Zarah felt claustrophobic as she stood at the foot of his bed. She knew what she had to do, but the thought of it terrified her.

The walls that held together her inner strength and courage came crumbling down. Her hands shook violently. Slowly, she approached him from the side. His eyes were closed and his breathing steady. She looked at the IV in his arm and saw that he was already receiving human blood in one thin tube, along with some type of clear medication in another. His ink-black shaggy hair hung loosely and framed his rugged, beautiful face.

With caution, she sat down beside him and

stared ahead at the too-white wall. Despite the shakiness that went all the way through to her bones, she could still feel every slight movement he made behind her. Every small breath and little twitch of his hands.

After less than a minute, Zarah knew he was awake without even turning around to look at him. She could sense it in the change of his breathing. He was indeed in pain. The poison was healing with the medication and human blood, but not fast enough.

"A Vampire's blood. He needs it. Soon. Or he will die."

Cathy's voice rang through her thoughts and Zarah clenched her eyes shut, trying to drown out the noise.

She was tainted. Something was wrong with her. Draven feeding from her would be too risky. The glowing thing that happened earlier reminded her that she was different—a freak. What if she fed him and it went terribly wrong? She couldn't just let him die though. Fear continued to boil in her, causing her heart to race.

"You keep shaking my bed like that, and I might vomit on you."

Draven's voice came out in a harsh, breathy rasp, barely above a whisper, but Zarah turned and forced a smile.

"Sorry."

He started to shrug, deciding against it when the pain wracked his body at the movement, wincing instead.

"What's wrong?" he asked when he saw her worried, cautious expression. A second later, the poison sent a sharp, stabbing convulsion through his body that sent him in a torturous buckling, groaning and crying out against the agony of it until the fit subsided. He was taking deep breaths and whispering hoarsely in curses when it was done. Zarah knew that was only the beginning, and she had to act quickly.

She shifted her eyes as tears began to form, struggling to get out the words.

Finally, after a moment's hesitation, Zarah thrust her wrist at Draven.

"You have to feed."

His eyes widened briefly, and then he rapidly shook his head.

"Hell no. I will not."

He tried to move away but was too weak and in too much pain.

"You have to," she repeated, pleading with her eyes.

"Not from you, I don't. If it's necessary for me to have vampire blood, then I'll wait." He turned his eyes away from her and closed them.

She was stung by his words, but shouldn't have been surprised. Dropping her arm back to her lap with a sigh, she turned and faced the wall again. Zarah guessed it was maybe for the best anyway that he didn't feed from her. The fears of whatever was going on still consumed her mind. She'd burned a Rogue to death with her bare hand that had *glowed*. Whatever that was about still baffled her.

"I figured," she whispered, the hurt almost clear in her words despite trying to mask it.

Another fifteen minutes passed and Zarah could hear Draven struggling more against the pain. He was going in and out of consciousness. His convulsions from the poison, the torture and stabbing aches that caused the agony were becoming more frequent. Whenever he'd buck and writhe within the sheets, howling, the beads of cold sweat traveling down his face, she'd turn and grip his upper shoulders to try and keep him as still as possible.

She didn't know how much longer she could sit idly by and watch the horror of his suffering. The other Guardians or Nathanial hadn't returned yet. He didn't really have the time to wait on them, either.

As his body shook again, her slender, shaking arms continued to try holding him down. She'd made her final decision then while watching his mouth twist in pain. That was it.

Zarah brought her wrist up to her mouth and took a sharp bite to open her vein. She placed it tenderly against Draven's lips, allowing the blood to drip past and onto his tongue. He was unconscious again, and she had to use her other hand to tilt his head up as she coaxed him.

"Come on," she whispered.

By instinct, seconds later, his fangs gripped her and he began to drink in gulps. Zarah gasped at the unexpected pain and excitement.

****

Draven could smell a mixture of pineapples and sweet lily flowers as he slowly came back into consciousness sometime later. A delicious liquid flowed over his tongue and he took deep drinks, savoring the flavors with a moan. Seconds passed and the fog began to lift from his mind, causing him to remember the night's events and where he was.

Popping his eyes open, he saw Zarah leaning over him. The scents were hers, and the taste that gloriously filled him flowed from the vein in her wrist, which she was still holding at his lips.

Zarah saw that he was awake, but didn't pull back. She waited for him to make the move, even though she knew that he'd taken enough, and she was exhausted. Her eyes were weary and she nearly slumped over him.

"What did you do?" He yanked himself away when he was fully aware. His voice was almost a shout, rough and laced with hints of growing agitation. He was definitely feeling better already.

She sluggishly moved off the bed and to the chair beside him. Without even a glance, Zarah shrugged and closed her eyes.

"I saved your ass. You can thank me later."

"No. I told you no earlier, and you still did it anyway!"

Opening her eyes and narrowing them in frustration, she turned her head toward him.

"You would have died, Draven. No one else has arrived back in time, and you wouldn't have made it waiting around. I'm not tainted, damn it. Don't worry, you're not going Rogue. You said yourself that you believed I was cured, remember?"

He glared at her and gritted his teeth. She saw his fists clench at his sides beneath the thin blanket, the muscles tensed in his shoulders.

Draven remained silent. Zarah's argument was not the reason why he was angry at her but he didn't want to tell her the truth. In a matter of minutes, the healing was taking place. His body felt warm, rich, and relaxed, causing a calm tiredness to fall over him. The convulsions and pain stopped. He could feel the silver poison being destroyed through the help of the medicine and her blood.

When he looked back at Zarah, she was on the verge of falling asleep, her eyelids still heavy and staring at him.

"What happened? I mean, uh, what happened back there with you? And how did we get out exactly?"

She barely lifted a shoulder in response. In truth, Zarah was in a bit of pain herself and wouldn't admit it. Her movements were stiff and exhaustion consumed her. The injuries she sustained were mild and could be slept off. They would also heal more once she fed.

"I don't know what happened—or how I burned that Rogue. That's just more questions to my already growing list, I guess. We got out with the help of Thomas. He gave me a chemical silver release bomb," she said in a whisper.

Draven tried to sit up from shock. Quickly refraining when he realized it was a bad idea as his head spun, he just shook his head.

"We haven't had those weapons in our

possession in—" he started.

"In about two years. And that's because Thomas was the Guardian that created them. When he went Rogue, they went with him," Zarah finished with a tired sigh.

"You're hurt." He observed. He stared up at the ceiling, avoiding eye contact. Her breathing was slow, shallow, and fatigued.
"I'll be fine."

Before long, she was asleep, curled into a tight ball on the plush, high-backed black fabric chair that sat beside Draven's bed. He fell back into unconsciousness shortly afterward as well, and there they both slept in peace next to each other—for once, neither being plagued by any dreams.

Twenty Two

"What happened?" Nathanial asked, striding into the hospital room. His eyes were frenzied, mouth set in a grim line.

"We were ambushed."

Draven sat up slowly, the thin paper blankets rustling and his mind still fuzzy. They both looked at Zarah, who still lay sleeping in the chair.

"You're both okay?" Nathanial asked. Draven nodded in response.

"Yeah, it was a tough fight. I'm surprised we even made it out alive. I don't even remember making it out. I think…I think she saved me, Sir," he stammered slowly. As the healing continued coursing through his veins, he knew he had just said the truth. Zarah had saved him.

"What do you mean?" His boss narrowed his eyes, suddenly looking dangerous.

The men didn't realize that beside them, Zarah was slowly coming awake to the sounds of their voices. Keeping her eyes closed and movements minimal, she listened to their hushed conversation.

"She fed me. No one else was here but her, and she saved me by giving me the blood I needed to cure the silver poisoning."

"She what?!" Nathanial froze at the foot of the bed with a shout. Anger was prevalent in his eyes and it startled Draven. His superior quickly composed himself and squared his shoulders back, running a shaky hand through his white hair.

"I'm sorry. I'm just concerned. I don't know if that was a good idea or not on her behalf to have done that."

Draven was silent for a moment before letting out a long breath and speaking with a slight stammer.

"I trust her. I don't believe any harm will come from it."

She sensed in his voice that perhaps he was trying to still convince himself of that idea. Her fingers twitched at her sides. One thing was certain, whether or not he hated her for doing it, she didn't have any regrets.

"Any harm? Draven, just last year she was Rogue…and she cured. There's something unusual about her, something otherworldly even for our kind. Now I can't help but have some concerns over whether or not she did something stupid by feeding you. In fact, I know she was stupid for it. She shouldn't have—" Nathanial prattled on through clenched teeth until Draven interrupted.

"Why the sudden change in opinion, Sir? If I remember correctly, it wasn't long ago when you first paired us up, that you told me I should never be concerned with her? Now you stand before me sounding like a hypocrite."

Zarah could hear the anger laced in her partner's voice, and the sound of Nathanial's gasp a mere foot from her chair told her that he had just been extremely offended as well. She didn't care. Draven was right in a way. Something was unusual in whatever it was that her boss was trying to say.

Silence passed for several heartbeats before Nathanial spoke again.

"So tell me then, did anything strange happen, or has happened, with her?"

"What do you mean?" Draven asked cautiously.

"For starters, there's something you should know. She's not entirely Vampire, Draven. Her mother was a Fallen Angel. And that can have some...effects. Of what exactly, I'm not entirely sure. She's the only half-breed of such in existence because Fallens and Vampires aren't exactly on good terms."

Zarah froze entirely in the chair. She held

her breath and kept her eyes tightly shut, too stunned at everything she was hearing. Half-breed? Fallen Angels?

What the hell?

Draven swallowed.

"No, I didn't know that, Sir." She could hear the lie in his trembling voice.

Apparently, Nathanial didn't though, because he continued on, pacing around the bed.

"Of course, only a very few people know this. Myself, her brother, and her father. Now you. Her father is dead. Thomas is Rogue and somewhere out there on the streets. I'm not stupid enough to believe that Thomas was destroyed. I suspect Zarah still secretly hunts for him, but there's nothing I can do to stop her from that. So, my question to you since you're around her most at this time is have you witnessed any strange occurrences from our unique Guardian? For example, unusual gifts that no other may possess?" Nathanial questioned flatly. He sounded now as if he were interrogating, rather than kindly checking up on them as he'd acted when he entered the room. It made her uncomfortable and she assumed that it was the same for her partner.

Another long silence passed and Zarah heard Draven shift again in the bed. This time it sounded as if he had sat completely up and was moving to get out.

"Perhaps, Nathanial. However, that isn't my business to discuss nor is this conversation one for me to be having with you. I think it's time for you to go. I'm beginning to feel better, thank you, but I believe Zarah still needs rest. She was under some extreme exhaustion already when we made it back." Draven was smooth, trying to cut the fury out of his voice as much as possible.

"Fine. But when you're both feeling better, I would like to have a meeting in my office. There's many things to discuss."

Nathanial swept from the room, the door closing softly behind him with an airtight seal.

Zarah remained silent with her eyes closed for several heartbeats as she let the conversation sink in. When she heard Draven let out a long sigh and the bed rustle while he stood, she blinked her eyes open slowly and stared at him.

He was slipping on his boots at the foot of the bed, not paying any attention to her. She noticed he still moved very cautiously while his body was trying to heal the wounds, but was recovering at an amazing speed. The bruises and cuts across his arms were faded, and the gash that had been in his side from the silver blade looked like nothing more than a large scratch. The stitches had already dissolved. Zarah was stunned at how fast he had healed from the poison. Was it because of her?

She caught herself staring at him. Her eyes roamed over his bare chest as he bent forward and tied his laces. His back stretched and she caught herself admiring his form.

"How much of that conversation did you hear?"

His voice startled her and she jumped, the soreness in her muscles screaming at her momentarily as she sat up in the chair with a sigh. He straightened up and looked at her through his intense blue eyes.

"Enough," she replied.
"Why did you lie about not knowing about my mother?"

Draven shrugged.
"He would have wanted to know how I knew, and I wouldn't have been able to explain."

"How did you know? I didn't even…" she started, stuttering, as she tried to force the tears back. Everything was just too much for her mind to comprehend at the moment, but she was trying. She was a half-breed. Fallen and Vampire. That's why she was so different. So what exactly did it all mean for her? Zarah still had many questions.

"Thomas told me."

Zarah met his eyes and saw the sympathy. No anger. No disgust. Her heart began to pound wildly in her chest as she went back to the thoughts of how emotionally-driven she became to save him earlier. There was a new bond between them.

"She was Fallen..." Zarah whispered. Leaning forward in the chair, she put her head in her hands and let the tears flow then. Draven rushed forward and knelt down, his hand brushing her back.

"That's why I'm wanted. That's what happened back there at the warehouse. I'm a new kind of species."

"You won't be alone for long, Zarah," Draven tried to soothe.

She looked up at him in confusion, her eyes red from the tears.

"I noticed while you were resting, before Nathanial came barging in. I had to hide my hands under the blankets while we were speaking because I don't know how to control it yet."

When he looked down at his hands, her eyes followed his to see that they were glowing a soft mix of silver and blue, fading in and out in a pulsing rhythm for a few seconds before the color fully stopped and his normal skin tone returned. A gasp escaped her lips and her eyes widened as she backed away from him.

"No…Draven…I'm so sorry…I should have never—" she started, worry and fear lacing her voice. Zarah had changed him with her blood. What was happening?

He shook his head and offered a smile.

"Don't be. You saved me. I don't know what's going on, but we'll figure it out. We'll go to Thomas and see if he knows anything."

She nodded warily, still unsure, as he handed her a bottle of blood so that she could start getting her strength back.

Just as she finished and felt her body reacting, healing, the nurse came in.

Draven sat back in the bed, the odd glowing having not returned since he started healing, and Zarah stood and started pacing around after getting her energy back.

"I see you're both feeling better already,"

Cathy said with a warm smile.

"You've recovered well. Draven, exceptionally fast."

She was handing them a couple of more bottles to put in the nearby miniature refrigerator to drink if they needed, and then checked over Draven's stats. She also gave Zarah a blanket and pillow to use if she wanted for rest.

"What time is it?" Zarah asked the nurse when she was about to leave the room again.

"Almost six."

Zarah frowned. The day had passed by in a blur and it was already almost nightfall again. Surely that was impossible? She must have slept a while earlier, and Nathanial must have taken his time before coming to visit. But nonetheless, the events they had endured had put them in the Compound hospital for the day and it made her restless then.

After the nurse left, Zarah turned to Draven with a sigh.

"Are you ready to go?"

"What? Where?" He uncrossed his ankles and sat up. He had been lying across the bed with shoes on, one arm tucked behind his head, ankles crossed, looking bored as he stared up at the ceiling in silence.

"I don't know. Anywhere. Probably to Thomas so I can get answers." Zarah shrugged.

Draven let out a long breath and began to shake his head in protest.

"No. You should rest. I don't think we'll go anywhere tonight."

She growled in frustration and flung herself down in the chair as he stared over at her with eyebrows raised in amusement. Huffing in annoyance, she let her breath blow the hair out of her face.

"You want to go get your cross-stitching?" He teased with a playful smile. She sent him an icy glare.

"I'm sorry—" he started, but before he could

get his sentence out was interrupted by a loud commotion outside of the hospital wing. Shots were ringing out through the hall, causing them to spring up from their spots.

Before they could reach the door, it flew open, and Zarah gasped.

Twenty-Three

"Thomas!" Zarah yelled.

Draven was beside her looking as surprised and shocked as her.

Behind her brother in the distance of the halls, they heard more gunshots and shouting. He was breathing heavily, out of breath and panting. She furrowed her brows at the outside commotion.

"What the hell is going on?" she asked, rushing forward. He threw weapons at them.

"No time to get into a detailed explanation, little sis," he replied as they began loading their guns.

"Be ready for war. The Rogues have overtaken the Compound. I'm here because I was with them when the Commander made the call to make the attack."

Zarah muttered a curse.

"How did they know the codes to get into the Compound to begin with?"

Thomas shrugged and she narrowed her eyes. Did her brother sell them out? The rage coiled around her as she stepped toward him.

"I swear, Thomas—" she started, only to be yanked back by Draven as he gripped her arm.

"We don't have time for this, Zarah. I trust this wasn't his doing, now let's drop it and get out of here before they reach you."

She turned and looked at him in surprise. His jaw was clenched in determination, eyes staring hard down at her.

"Leave? Are you saying that we just leave while the Guardians fight for their lives out there against who-knows how many Rogues? It could be a losing battle, Draven. We should be helping." She shook her arm free of his grasp and stepped away from him.

"They're after you. They know what you did at the warehouse, and they're here to get you once and for all. Draven is right. You need to get out of here," Thomas cut in.

"No!" she turned and screamed.

Zarah stormed up to Thomas in the doorway, Draven a few steps behind her trying to protest but to no avail. She wasn't going to listen. She was going to fight. She was not a Guardian who ran away. Not anymore at least.

"Move," she demanded. She was almost a foot shorter than him but it didn't intimidate her.

When Thomas remained silent and stood there stubbornly, she raised her gun and pointed it in his face with a feral growl.

"I said move, Thomas. You can help me fight, or you can get shot. Your choice."

His red eyes narrowed and finally after a moment's silence, stepped aside.

"Don't think that I'm doing this because I'm afraid of you, either. It's only because I know you'll need the help. The Guardians are outnumbered."

As he said that, more screaming echoed around them and the smell of smoke began to fill the air. They ran out of the room and toward the main lobby where the commotion was, passing fallen Guardians along the way.

"Where's Nathanial?" Draven shouted over the noise as they drew closer to the fighting, now beginning to get caught up in the action.

A lone Rogue that had been standing guard at their end of the hall caught sight of them and began to charge. Zarah raised her gun and fired, the bullet striking the angry monster's head and throwing him backwards through a wall. He hadn't even had time to let out a warning at her.

She turned back to Draven and shrugged.

"I don't see him around here at least. Maybe

he's fighting somewhere, or locked in his office."

More gunshots fired out caught their attention again. Zarah glanced at Thomas.

"Are you sure you're with us?" Her eyes were suspicious. Sure he had been helping her and Draven a lot recently, but she still didn't know if she could fully trust him sometimes.

He clenched his fists and let out a throaty grumble.

"Of course I am."

She nodded.

"Alright then, just making sure. Don't let another Guardian kill you because I might not always be able to keep an eye on you. Killing you is my job, remember."

With that, she started forward, gun ready.

The guys looked at each other momentarily, eyebrows raised, before turning and following her into the fight.

****

The fighting was intense the further they crowded into the Compound's main lobby near the elevators. Zarah looked around at the scene.

The place was trashed.

Resident Guardians were fighting with all the strength they could muster, Rogues were coming in by masses through the elevator from the above parking garage, and fires from various rooms had erupted. Blood splashed on the walls caused Zarah to have flashes of scenes she'd fought to keep at the back of her mind. She grabbed at her temple and clenched her eyes shut with trembling lips. The screams and laughter roared through her in waves. She heard bodies flying, hitting objects with sickening crunches, but when she opened her eyes everything still moved in a blur. Her nostrils flared and her eyes widened in fear.

"Watch out!" she heard a vaguely familiar voice shout. Her hearing sounded tunneled through all the chaos. She thought it was Thomas, and spun around in time.

She ducked as a rabid charged at her, causing his fist to get stuck in the wall. Her instincts came back in a rush. Without so much as a blink of her eye, she took her silver dagger from her belt loop and stabbed him through his back, reaching his heart, before he could turn around and attack again.

Draven wasn't far away fighting a pair, too. When they'd entered the fight, she hadn't even had time to tell him to take it easy before the army descended upon them. She began to silently worry that maybe she had made a mistake in wanting to join the fight after all, looking around as she spotted Thomas and Alyssa as well. She noticed her partner and the two Rogues fighting together within minutes, sharing weapons, and her heart swelled with a sudden, unexpected pride.

Fighting her way through the crowd, she made her way toward them. If she was going to die, it'd be by their side.

"You're even lovelier in person."

A Rogue stepped in front of Zarah, causing her to freeze.

"Oh? Yeah, I'm sure you've heard so much about me," she replied with a smirk, holding her gun tight.

Her eyes wandered over to Draven, who was also staring at her in worry and trying to get to her. Except that he and her brother were beginning to come under attack by a large group and couldn't escape the foray to help her.

Zarah looked around and frowned when seeing that many of the other Guardians had been left on the floor, wounded, dead or simply gone. It was only them against the army then.

This didn't look good at all.

"I've heard a lot about you actually. The Commander sends his regards. He wished he could be here tonight, but he wanted to be ready for when I brought you in instead."

The Rogue's voice brought her attention back to him and she stared in disbelief.

"I'm not going anywhere with you. Don't flatter yourself."

She started to raise her gun, noting that he had no weapon, and walk toward Draven while motioning him to go to the elevators. When she reached him, she saw they were surrounded on all sides, making it hard to leave.

"I think you will," the Rogue commented across from her, smirking.

The army attacked, blood-thirsty monsters lunging at them from all sides, and they had barely little time to react. Many of these were less intelligent—the Rogues that had yet to be bitten or drink from one of the more "conscious" beings. These were the monsters that Zarah used to hunt before her world went crazy.

Their weapons were running short, while the numbers of Rogues were growing larger. Zarah tried to keep her focus on the fight, but her vision strayed occasionally to Draven. He was beginning to get tired she knew since he was still recovering from the previous fight.

They were separating. Drifting farther and farther away into a battle against several Rogues at a time and Zarah knew this was their plan. When the fire started in the midst of their battle, her breath caught. Her eyes scanned the area frenzied and distressed more for her partner's safety. That moment of weakness cost her.

"You really are quite a beauty."

She tried to turn to face the Rogue, but he had his iron grip on her. He kept her facing forward, her eyes focused on Draven who was still oblivious to the situation. His hands wound around to her stomach and pulled her closer against his body. While he smelled of cinnamon and coffee, Zarah wanted to lose all the contents of her stomach just from the filth of his touch.

She felt a tingling sensation in her hands and started to smile, only for the Rogue to growl in her ear.

"Turn it off or they all die right now."

She looked down and saw that her hands had begun to glow, that same soft violet glow as before, and the Rogue behind her was instructing her to turn the ability off. Zarah didn't even know what was going on with her, much less, how did he?

Sighing, she closed her eyes and thought about it.

"How do I know you're not going to kill them anyway?" she finally whispered back.

"We only came for you. Now turn it off. We leave, and they'll be left." His voice held authority. She could tell he was the leader of this mission. He snaked one of his hands upward into her hair at the base of her neck. It made her shudder.

"I see the way you look at him. I know you don't want him hurt."

She opened her eyes and stared across at Draven again. He was fighting beside her brother and Alyssa. Clenching her jaw tight, she made every effort to stop whatever it was that was causing the strange aura. She was going to save them at least.

"I don't know how," she growled. Her anger made the heat intensify, causing the Rogue to let out a short yelp.

"It's called concentration, my dear. Turn it off or in one single instruction, I will have them destroyed. And don't think about doing it anyway. It won't save you either. If I die, they're automatically instructed to kill."

Stop. She kept thinking to herself. Finally with some struggle, she calmed herself and the light faded, and the Rogue seemed to let out a sigh of relief behind her. Zarah began to wonder if she'd made a mistake, but then it was too late as he yanked a needle from his pocket and plunged it into her neck.

She screamed.

Draven turned from the fight and they met each other's eyes. His widened, first in shock, then in horror.

"Zarah!"

As the three of them tried to run toward her, she could feel her consciousness slipping. The Rogue kept one arm around her, motioning the others to begin their retreat out of the Compound with the other.

Thomas and Alyssa were tossed through a bedroom door where a fire raged. Draven was picked up by his shirt collar and thrown against a wall, his head slamming back and causing his balance to falter. Before he could recover and pick himself up, a heavy bookshelf fell in front of him. A couple more fires ignited around him and laughter rang out as he struggled to get up.

Zarah's vision was slowly becoming fuzzy. The sounds around her distorted. The room spun in and out of focus. She kept whispering for Draven under her breath but no one heard her.

As she was being dragged out by the Rogue with the others following, laughing menacingly around her, she could hear Draven faintly in the distance over the disorienting noise until she finally succumbed to unconsciousness.

He was screaming her name.

Twenty Four

Draven started coughing. There was too much smoke. With his head spinning wildly and his legs taking some time to push his body up from the wall, he looked around at the damage.

The Compound was destroyed.

And Zarah was gone.

"Thomas!" he began to shout, pushing through piles of trash, stepping around burning books and destroyed computer systems that lay scattered along the tiled floor.

"We're here."

Draven breathed a silent sigh of relief when seeing the Rogue and his mate come stumbling from the room they had been tossed into, also coughing from the heavy smoke. He rushed over to them and they all looked around in silence.

Movement suddenly caught their attention in one corner of the room, causing Draven to draw his gun in a flash and steadily move to the area.

"It's just me," a hoarse voice said after debris had been kicked away from his body. It was a Guardian, injured but alive.

"Jerry?" Thomas breathed out in surprise. The Guardian was rising to his feet, slowly moving. Upon hearing Thomas' voice, he snapped his attention to him and his jaw dropped.

"Thomas? But it can't be... You're—" he started, stuttering in disbelief. His eyes shifted warily to Thomas' eyes, noting the red irises. As he swallowed a lump in his throat, he began to reach for his gun.

Seeing the situation, Draven quickly stepped

in front of Zarah's brother and shook his head.

"No. He's on our side. There's no time to explain right now. Just trust me."

The Guardian hesitated; his hand wavered over his weapon while he stared hard at Draven, before nodding.

"Alright."

So at least they had Jerry on their team as they began to search the Compound for more survivors and come up with a plan to go save Zarah.

****

"And you're sure that's where they're going to be?" Draven asked, eyeing Thomas timidly.

"Yeah. That was the plan. I hope, anyway, that things didn't change as soon as they realized I was fighting against them. It doesn't hurt to go check at least, right?"

Draven looked down at his watch. They

couldn't afford to waste much time so he nodded in agreement with Thomas.

"Right."

During the brief check of the Compound, they had found three other surviving Guardians along with Jerry. Many were dead, and a few were missing. Nathanial was among the missing. They'd managed to get the fires out with a few fire extinguishers, but due to the extent of damage, had to take refuge in the Lounge. It was the only place in the Compound that hadn't been critically hit, as well as the gym.

After convincing the survivors to help, they had formed a small team to prepare a rescue mission. Thomas informed them that the Rogue army and the Commander could be at an old abandoned military base on the outskirts of the city.

Standing around the pool table in the Lounge, he looked at the team that had assembled. There were six of them in all including himself. The odds were going to be bad and he knew it, but he would risk it to save her.

"Let's go."

He attached several rounds of ammunition to his vest, two pistols in holsters, and a large silver dagger in a case at his hip as the others followed suit. They had stocked up on weapons during their sweep of the building.

"We're going on a suicide mission, Draven," one of the Guardians said as they headed out. It was James, at one time was his pool-playing buddy.

They all entered the elevator and headed up toward the parking garage. Draven turned to the young Guardian, his face full of determination and rage, his frame dominating compared to his.

"Maybe. But I'm going to save her."

"You'll probably die trying, just like we all will," James hissed back. At that moment, the elevator doors opened, and as they did, the rage so carefully controlled inside of Draven snapped. He yanked the Guardian forward by the straps of his vest and threw him outside onto the concrete with a snarl.

"If you want to be a coward, then go! Get out of here, because I certainly don't have time to mess with your foolishness!" he screamed furiously. An old couple passing by in the garage stopped briefly to stare. They all grew silent for a few heartbeats until Jerry casually stepped forward with usual charming smile.

"How are you lovely folks doing tonight? That's good... We're just some military brats—" He led them away some distance toward their car, out of sight. They were making eye contact constantly with him. The others could taste the mysticism in the air: Jerry was hypnotizing the elderly couple to believe they hadn't seen anything.

Thomas reached forward and touched Draven's arm tentatively, his eyes widened in shock. James was also starting to stand, a look of disbelief on his face as well.

"Draven," Thomas started.

"You're..." and then he stopped, quickly

pulling his hand away.

"What?"

"Cold. And I don't mean the normal kind of cold for our kind. Just look at yourself."

Draven looked down at his hands and gasped.

In the darkness of the garage, he emitted a faint silver aura. He approached the metal elevator doors again and used them for a mirror. It faded in the instant that his emotions calmed, but his eyes remained the same, and they had changed in the last forty-eight hours. No longer a solid bright blue, they were a multitude of colors swirling together. His blue was the dominate color, but within the depths of his irises now danced a swirling mixture of gold and violet flecks.

"What the hell is going on?" he whispered, mostly to himself, touching his cheeks with awe.

"You've been changed because of her," a sudden strange voice boomed from behind them all at the entrance of the garage.

Turning, they were all met with an unexpected sight. There stood eight Fallens in formation and geared for a battle. Their full, towering frames blocked out much of the light from the nearby streetlamps. Gold eyes glowed and glared at the six of them through the darkness as if they were being scrutinized mentally, and their large, black wings were tucked neatly behind them.

Draven swallowed nervously, unsure of the situation.

Then the Fallen in front, a six and a half foot tall, muscled man with long blonde-red hair, stepped forward and turned his gaze toward Thomas. He must have been the leader, Draven assumed, the one who had spoken the first time to get their attention.

"Thomas, we've come to fight as a favor to your mother. A last request of hers that we shall honor."

The Fallen folded his fist and placed it over

his heart to show a sign of protection and honor, the others followed his action quickly after.

Draven felt a smug smile tug at the corner of his mouth. Perhaps now they had more of a fighting chance against the Rogue army after all. Turning back to James who was now standing at the back of their group, he smirked.

"Are you with us now?"

Twenty Five

Zarah awoke to find herself wrapped in darkness. She was lying on cold concrete and strong silver cuffs were locked securely around her wrists.

When she tried to move her arms, she found that the cuffs were linked to chains that had been hooked somewhere into a nearby wall. No matter how much she tried to struggle, she couldn't break them. Her body was too weak, her mind still fuzzy and spinning from the drugs coursing through her body. Even her vision was still blurred as she continued trying to adjust her sight to her surroundings.

"Well it looks like our Sleeping Beauty awakens," a husky voice broke through the eerie, dark silence near her. She recognized it immediately, jumping from her spot on the cold floor and trying to back against the wall behind her.

Her head was swimming again and her vision still wouldn't focus well enough to adjust to see her surroundings. She could only feel the concrete beneath her shaking body and the smooth concrete wall behind her back. The cuffs on her wrists were attached to chain that led to something holding her in place, but still allowing her some movement. Even though with every move she made, her muscles screamed, tense and sore, and her head spun and ached.

Zarah heard the footsteps approaching then. She knew it was the same Rogue who had snatched her from The Compound, the one who had stabbed her with the needle and drugged her with whatever it was coursing through her system at that time.

"Tranquilizer mixed with a dose of sedative. It put you out for quite a while, and I didn't mean for that to happen. I only meant for it to drug you up some. Guess I had too much tossed in," he said as if he'd read her thoughts. That would certainly explain her drug-induced state. Most human drugs didn't affect their kind, and in order for them to, it would take an extremely high dose or a mixture.

She jumped when his hand touched her cheek.

"Is it you?" She finally found her voice, hoarse and dry.

"Are you really The Commander?" Somehow, Zarah knew the answer before he even responded. The Rogue before her was merely a pawn. A powerful one.

He laughed. The image of him kneeling in front of her was slowly coming into her focus, a bit blurry as her eyes tried to adjust.

"No. You'll meet him soon enough."

"The Commander told me something interesting about you..." he started after a moment's silence.

Zarah held her breath. The Rogue brandished a silver dagger and began to trace a line down her jaw, careful not to break skin. Chills erupted up her spine and she shivered.

"...You carry great power because of your blood. He said you'll create a new race," his voice was barely above a whisper as he continued, breathing deeply and close to her ear as she began to struggle against her restraints.

She let out a cry when the blade dug deeper into her skin. The stinging sensation followed by the burn and dizzy spells that overcame her told her senses that the silver poisoning was slowly working its way into her system. She fought hard and remained focused as she watched him pull the dagger back to him. He smirked at the sight of her blood.

"I don't u-understand," Zarah stammered.

"What is there not to understand? You're special! You will be building a new race of Vampires with your blood. It's called Elemental

Magick. It's a part of a Fallen's power. I know you've felt it, and can still feel it within you even there in your drug induced mind. Why else do you think we wanted you?" The Rogue was laughing, staring at her with cold, red eyes.

"I thought you just wanted a cure." She thought she could be stalling by keeping him in a conversation. At the same time, she was learning information that she had wanted to know more about. No matter how hard it was hearing it.

He laughed harder and shook his head.

"Rumor. We weren't after any particular cure. We just wanted your blood. Plain and simple."

"The humans will overpower you, either way. They have an extensive military system. And chaos will cause people to do outrageous things. Vampires will never rule over the human world. It will be constant war."

Zarah was growing weaker, the silver getting deeper into her system from the cuts.

"War we can win, Zarah. Especially with a new race."

She saw the look in his eyes, the bright red flash of desire and hunger, and began to shake her head frantically.

"No," she tried to plead but it barely came out in a whisper.

When he pinned her up against the wall and turned her head to the side, his body pressed against hers and his breath hot on her neck, she managed to let out the scream just before his fangs plunged into her flesh.

"No!"

****

Draven and the others had walked to the base instead of trying to take a multitude of cars. They figured it would be a better form of attack.

"Are you sure this is it?" Draven turned to

Thomas and asked when they reached the outside fence. Looking in, the place looked dark and deserted. There weren't even any Rogues standing guard around the doors like they'd assumed.

"Yeah, I'm sure."

With a sigh, they each began climbing over the chain-link fencing, landing quietly in the grass on the other side before making their way along the shadows behind old buildings toward the largest. They followed Thomas from that point.

"What did you mean, back there at the garage, that she had…changed…me?" Draven asked in a whisper to the Fallen, whose name he had learned to be Seth.

Seth looked down at him with a frown as if he were thinking on how best to explain it.

"Fallens are gifted with special powers for defense. It's called Elemental Magick. Fire, Earth, Water, Spirit, Wind, Ice. We don't have the power to use them all. Some powerful ones can, but most not. Seems you have Ice, or perhaps both Water and Ice since the two Elements can combine easily. The Fallen, and her mother, weren't sure that Zarah was ever going to develop that defense, though, since she's a Halfling."

"And she passed it on to me? Because I fed from her?" Draven asked in shock.

Seth nodded.

"Zarah can be dangerous in her own way, Draven. She can create a whole new race of Vampires if she wanted. I'm not sure if it's even safe that she is alive."

Thomas stepped in between them and stared at Seth, his eyes dark and angry.

"Stay away from my sister." His voice was warning enough.

"Are you forgetting that I and my guards are here to help?"

"I'm not. But what are the plans once this battle is over?" Thomas asked through narrowed eyes.

"That we will see about."

"Yes, we will certainly see."

With the exchange finished, Thomas turned on his heels and started for the base again. Everyone had grown quiet during the tension.

When they arrived toward the front, they looked around in confusion. It was quiet and still dark.

"Thomas, I'm really not sure this is right—" Draven began with a frustrated sigh.

"Oh, it's right, Guardian," a sudden voice said nearby, laughing.

They all turned, drawing their weapons at the same time, and met the Rogue that had taken Zarah from The Compound. He was casually leaning against a side door with a smirk plastered on his face. His eyes caught Draven's attention immediately.

They weren't red.
They were silver.

"He knows where Zarah is," Draven growled to Thomas and began to head toward the Rogue.

Just then, one of the bay garage doors opened and the army of Rogues began to charge out for the fight. In a final glance before joining the fight, the Rogue with the silver eyes waved a farewell from the side door before disappearing. This caused Draven to let out a roar of anger.

"Go!" Thomas yelled.
"Go on, we'll hold the fight out here!"

"Who is that?" Draven asked, shooting a nearby Rogue in the head.

"His name is Ethan. He's the one who turned me Rogue. If you find him, send him my regards."

Draven nodded and then turned and headed toward the side door where Ethan had disappeared.

Twenty Six

When Draven stepped into the base, it was dark save for a few small fluorescent lamps scattered in a couple of far corners. The garage was huge. He could tell it had once been an old airplane hangar, probably having held several military crafts at one time along with trucks. It was empty now, though, and every sound echoed around him.

"You'll lose, Guardian."

Draven's attention snapped toward Ethan's voice in the dark, his nerves tensed and gun held steady. The Rogue, or whatever he was now since Draven couldn't even determine what he was himself, was smirking at him from a windowsill.

"Where is she, Ethan?" Draven asked with a hiss, raising the gun.

Ethan let out a dark chuckle.

"So you know who I am. I figured all along that Thomas was working with the two of you. He's special, too. Did you know that?"

Draven hesitated and looked at him in confusion.

"Maybe he doesn't even know it because he's always thought it was just Zarah. But their mother was apparently very powerful, and she passed something along to each of them. Thomas brought our mentality back, our mind, our control. Zarah holds the Elemental Magick. Quite interesting, don't you think, Guardian?" Ethan continued chatting as if there wasn't a gun with a silver bullet pointed at his head.

Draven's curiosity won out and his thoughts wavered. Ethan was handing out information. Perhaps something important he should know.

"What do you mean Thomas brought the

Rogues back to intelligence? He became Rogue after you already were intelligent or do you not remember how you and your gang ambushed him and Zarah one night? That's how he was turned. Zarah remembers it," he snapped.

"Ah, yes. But it was his blood. The Commander brought a vial of the Guardian Thomas' blood to me shortly after I became Rogue and fed it to me. Once it was in my system, I became intelligent. From there, whenever I turned any Vampire or a Rogue fed from me, they became intelligent. It's also how I found Thomas. I remembered his scent and his taste."

Ethan winked. Draven growled.

"Where is Zarah?"

"That is a question I'll be happy to answer. She is in the room at the end of this garage meeting with The Commander. He threw me out when he caught me breaking his rules."

Draven frowned and kept the weapon pointed him as he slowly started walking toward the back of the garage, toward the door that Ethan was directing him to. His eyes met Ethan's and he was reminded again of what must have happened to Zarah.

"You fed from her. How should I believe you that she's even alright?"

"She was fine when I was thrown out. I only took enough for this, no harm done. I can't make any guarantees as to her condition now that she's there with The Commander though."

"Why are you just letting me waltz in here and telling me where to go? Shouldn't you be guarding? Or attacking or something?" Suspicion laced Draven's words.

"Hey man, you have the guns. Besides don't you hear it in the background?" Ethan had a crazy personality. Perhaps he was mentally unstable even before having gone Rogue, however long ago that had been.

Draven stopped moving and listened. Yes, suddenly he heard it. Over the sound of the fighting outside, he could hear the coming sirens in the distance. A helicopter was flying in also and would be landing somewhere outside the base within the next few minutes. Heavy armored trucks were clamoring up the road nearby. Humans. His heart was racing as he stared at Ethan in shock, who continued sitting on the window, now wearing a sly smile.

"The whole world is about to change in just a matter of hours. I'll be seeing you again soon, I'm sure. Tell Zarah I might repay her sometime for at least curing me," Ethan said. In a blink, he dropped from the window and disappeared.

With no time to bother chasing after him, Draven turned back and tried to head toward the door that Ethan had directed him to at the back of the base. That's where he would find Zarah he was told. A spark of hope rose in his chest.

That hope sizzled when a gang of Rogues

stepped out from the shadows. Obviously they had left the outside fight and followed him in to protect The Commander. Looking around at the group, he counted twelve. They sneered mockingly forming a half-circle around him, blocking his way to the door.

Draven's emotions churned and anger boiled into rage. He was not going to let the monsters stop him from reaching Zarah. Staring hard at the group, he noticed their wide-eyed shock and then looked down at his hands to see the silver aura returned. A smirk turned up his lips. She had gifted him with a power he could use for fighting. He would learn to control it and use it to his advantage. Especially in that moment.

Glaring again at the group around him, he saw that they were no longer interested in whatever strange new thing he was. Only that he was trying to get to their leader and they had to stop him. The monsters were preparing for an attack. And better for him that they didn't have any weapons. Rogues had always been a bit "old school" in that style of fighting. With the exception of Thomas, who loved his little Glock. If anything at all, the Rogues may carry silver knives at the most.

When the attack began, Draven holstered his gun and smiled darkly. The silver aura glowed brighter around him and he could feel the power drawing up from his center. He would likely be fighting without his weapons as well.

"So cold..." a Rogue barely whispered, shivering and choking, as Draven held him by the throat high in the air above him.

"...Your eyes..."

Draven continued to watch in silence until the Rogue in his hand was frozen. Then with a loud *Snap!* his head broke away from his shoulders and fell, shattering into tiny shards of ice on the concrete floor at his feet.

It had all seemed to have happened in slow motion, but everything was blurring from happening in only a matter of seconds.

When Draven turned after dropping the

frozen body of the Rogue, he was met with two more attacking his back. He couldn't react in time to get a grip on either one, or reach for his holster, as they both charged and body slammed him into the wall. Seconds later, gunshots fired and the two in front of him fell from wounds to their heads. He looked up and almost sighed in relief.

"Didn't think I would completely abandon you in here, now did you, Guardian?" Thomas asked with a smirk before he joined the fight.

****

Zarah's consciousness was clouded. She was in and out of a constant stupor, noting the silver restraints still bound on her wrists to keep her in place.

She tried hard to remember the small details. Why she was there? What had happened?

Her body shook from the poison dwelling in her bloodstream. A sharp pain throbbed in her neck. And when she regained her full sense of awareness, the memories all came rushing back to her.

The Rogue had attacked her, though not viciously. It was almost as if he tried to be tender. Surely not? When her screams had finally subsided from the surprise, she saw through his eyes, having seen all the darkness that resided through him. It made her shudder in fear. She'd realized who he was. He'd been the one to change Thomas rabid. She didn't get the time to discuss that.

Then *he* came. The Commander.

"Ethan!" a low growl sounded from somewhere in the room. Before she could blink to focus on the figure floating toward them, the Rogue was ripped away from her and thrown across the room where she heard a lot of crashing.

"You idiot!" he boomed.
"I strictly forbade anyone from touching her until I arrived!"

Zarah watched through drooping eyes, her head bobbing to the side as she continued to lose blood and fight the poison in her system. The Commander, cloaked again as before, was standing above her with his back facing her. She heard Ethan let out a dark chuckle and saw that he lay in a pile of rubble where he'd been thrown against the far wall. Blood dribbled from his mouth onto his chin. Some of it had been hers.

"Do you really think that you're the one who's going to bring this world to its knees? You're too old. They need someone fresh. Besides, I might want a queen. And she's quite lovely on the eyes. Tasty, too."

Her stomach churned. She had no idea what was going on, but her insides felt ready to expel at any moment.

Ethan stood from the rubble and swayed, holding his head in his hands.

"Whoa."

He began to shake. Clutching tightly at his temple and squeezing his eyes shut, Ethan stumbled along the wall and tried to remain steady on his feet. The air in the room was feeling electric and from somewhere deep within her, something swelled with power. A fuse was waiting to be ignited, but Zarah still didn't understand what exactly was happening.

She watched him as best as she could, her eyesight going hazy but still there enough to see him. Swallowing, she thought briefly that at one time, Ethan would have been handsome before going Rogue. He was tall with curly blonde hair and leanly muscled. Then he lifted his head while still holding it, frowning as if he had nothing left but an exhausting headache, and she saw his eyes.

They were no longer red.
They were silver.

The Commander growled and charged him. Zarah started to shout. She wanted to know what happened. All she knew was that whatever it was, it was because he had fed from her. Before she went unconscious, she saw them fighting—yelling at each other mostly about power and standings and herself, and then she heard a helicopter somewhere in the distance. Fear sparked in her chest. Humans were going to know. The world was going to change.

She could hear fighting somewhere outside, but it couldn't be. Her mind was confused, fuzzy. Zarah thought maybe she was just hearing things. Maybe she was just imagining the helicopter, too. She tried to hope.

Then the hood of The Commander's cloak fell and she gasped.
"Nathanial!" she breathed before the blackness took her.

After the memories flooded her when she regained her consciousness, she looked around, hoping against hope that it hadn't been Nathanial she'd seen as her enemy. But it dimmed when she saw him standing at the far end of the room near a table. Ethan was gone. She didn't know if Nathanial had killed him, or if he had just simply left. At that moment, she didn't care. She only thought of the situation she was in and the man that was in the room with her then.

"You were like a father to me. How could you betray me like this?" she croaked, hating the weakness that overtook her as tears sprang to her eyes.

Nathanial turned to face her with a rueful smile.

"No, Zarah, I was like a father to you so you would trust me. So that I could betray you now. It's time for our species to rise up in this world. Humans are inferior to us, and you are a special gift to our kind. Rogues are like cockroaches. You can help change them, all the while we can gain our rightful place in the world. A new species entirely sounds rather enticing."

She swallowed hard.

"Ethan said it wasn't about a cure."

"Not entirely, no. It's a process during the change of creating the new species from your blood, though, so… Two for the price of one, I guess you can say."

Zarah sucked in a sharp breath.

"I've lived at The Compound all this time. Why didn't you just make your move then?" she suddenly snapped, angry.

"Because I had to be sure that you were going to develop any of the Fallen traits. Once I was sure, that's when I began to make my plans. I started with Thomas, my dear. The ambush on you and him that night he was turned Rogue. That was my doing. It was Ethan who turned your brother and he was already intelligent because I stole a vial of your brother's blood from the hospital wing and fed it to him."

When her eyes widened in surprise, he continued in a low growl, stepping closer to her.

"You see, Zarah, even Thomas had some traits passed onto him from your filthy Fallen mother. His body could fight the Rogue virus hard, but not strong enough to cure. He would still be lost to the bloodlust—having the same red eyes, same malicious need to attack and drain humans—but he would be better controlled and continue to keep his mind intact. I noticed this after viewing his blood samples several times, interacting it with Rogue blood samples, until I finally fed Ethan with his blood and he went intelligent just as I'd expected. I wanted to test you, but there was only one way I wanted to test you. So I set up the ambush, and waited patiently for Thomas to seek you out and turn you himself. Everything happened exactly as I'd expected."

Zarah could feel her building fury and hurt. He did it. He caused it all. Thomas being Rogue, his turning her…the loss of that human group she brutally murdered and is haunted by in her dreams. All. Of. It.

She tried to pump her fists and to pull at the restraints but her arms were heavy and she was tired.

"How could you?" she asked, out of breath. He was approaching her with something in his hand and she was getting dizzy again.

"Simple. I hate Fallens and I hate humans. Create a new species with your kind of power and we could rule them all."

"Or they will hunt us all down like a game. You don't think about shit, Nathanial," she hissed.

He didn't respond. His eyes were too crazed as he knelt down in front of her. She saw what was in his hand then and tried to back away, only striking wall.

He had a needle.

Gripping her arm roughly, he brought it forward and found her vein at the crook of her elbow. With a yelp, she felt the needle glide in and then saw blood flow into the vial behind it. He looked into her eyes and smirked.

Twenty Seven

Nathanial had five small glass vials of Zarah's blood before he stopped. Her stomach clenched again. He was harvesting her blood to use and it made her nauseous. She rolled her head back against the wall in exhaustion.

Setting the vials down on the table, he came back to her and patted her head. She winced and shrank away from his touch, disgusted.

"I heard you fed Draven. I'll just have to dispose of him later. He's too attached now. I should have never forced that Bonding Pact, I guess. That was a mistake on my part. I thought I could have him keep an eye on you without worrying about any kind of affection."

"There's not any affection there." She heard

the doubt in her own voice. He laughed loudly and shook his head.

"I'm not that stupid."

Her emotions peaked thinking of him. She wondered briefly if he was alright. He had been caught in that fire at The Compound just before Ethan had drugged her and taken her away. Swallowing nervously, she watched Nathanial in silence as he glided around the room, playing with her vials of blood, no longer paying attention to her.

"And me? What are you going to do with me now that you have what you want?" she wondered out loud after an awkward pause. Pain snaked through her body each time she talked, and her head spun wildly, but she continued to fight to stay awake, afraid that if she fell into unconsciousness one more time she may not wake again.

He turned slightly, staring over his shoulder. No emotion showed on his face.

"You will die in the morning sun or given over to the humans. Whichever comes first." Then he shrugged.

She raised her head and that's when she noticed the small window at the top of the back wall. It wasn't big, not enough to have fit a body, but big enough to let in the outside light. At her angle, it would let in just the right amount of sunlight to hit and burn her to a slow death. She started to struggle against the restraints again.

"It's no use to fight. The drugs and silver poison in your system have made you too weak," he sneered.

"You can't even bring out your Elemental power, I made sure of that."

With that, he turned back to what he was doing at the table. She saw him take a vial, open it, and drink it down as her tired eyes widened in horror. Nathanial couldn't get a power. He wouldn't control it.

Through the chaos of her mind, she heard everything again. There was definitely fighting outside somewhere. Shouting. Shooting.

She heard him somewhere close by the closed

door of the room she was in. Draven's voice. He shouted something intangible on the other side of the wall. It sounded distant, faint, but it was definitely him. She sucked in a sharp breath. Her hand slapped the wall in a weak attempt to pull herself up.

Strange warmth blossomed in her chest. Determination gave her an unexplainable strength, and before she could react, the silver cuffs broke silently from her wrists. Nathanial hadn't noticed. He was too busy frowning in confusion at the empty vial in his hands.

"Nothing's happening." He mumbled out loud to himself, still ignoring her, and then she knew. In order for a change to take place, one would have to feed directly from her or another Elemental. Not a tainted glass vial that had been diluted with air pollutants or metal.

She smiled slyly at her freedom and Nathanial's ignorance, approaching him with the grace of a cat. She could feel her power, immense and flowing in waves over her body. Her fangs extended in excitement.

She tapped his shoulder and he spun wildly. When seeing her he was dumbfounded, unable to find his words. She gave him no time to react, reaching out in blinding speed without a word, to grip him by his throat.

"Of course it won't work. You're not worthy," she seethed with clenched teeth. She saw that her body glowed again, this time a much brighter violet. She almost laughed in spite of everything when seeing the aura. It reminded her of neon. He choked on whatever response he tried to give.

She smiled, evil yet beautiful, and then tossed him through the door with such an extreme force it burst apart from the hinges and frame, sending chunks of wall plaster and twisted metal soaring out with him, before following his flying body out of the room.

****

Draven was in the midst of fighting, with Thomas nearby, when his attention was brought to the back of the bay after a large crash came tumbling through the door of the room where he knew Zarah was. A scream as a flying body landed through the rubble of concrete and steel echoed around them.

And then there she was.

Zarah stood in the doorway with a vicious smile curving her lips. A bright violet aura surrounded her body, and her eyes glowed vividly. He saw the faint cut on her cheek and could sense not only the silver poisoning in her system, but the intense power that fought around it through her emotions.

He looked down at the body in the rubble and his own enraged emotions boiled over upon seeing who The Commander had been. Nathanial. A low rumble erupted from his chest as he thought of the betrayal. A snarl escaped between his teeth and his lip curled up in loathing.

Zarah hadn't seen Draven. She only had her focus on Nathanial as she stepped over the rubble toward him. He struggled to stand. With a simple wave of her hand, she used a magical force to lift him in the air, causing him to shout in alarm. Wind began to howl around them, kicking up dust and debris into a cyclone.

Draven continued to fight through the attacking Rogues, using his own power and silver daggers as he slashed away or froze them with a single touch. All the while, his attention strayed to watch her.

The wind she had brought on whipped her long hair around her face and as she dropped the breezing cyclone around her, he could see through the falling dust that she was gripping Nathanial by his throat against the wall. She stood an arm's length away from him. The glow from her aura was even brighter than before.

He swallowed. Fear and admiration consumed him.

Zarah looked like a goddess.

During his lapse of attention on the surrounding fight, he felt a sharp pain in his arm and looked down. A Rogue had managed to get in a strike, making a small gash at his shoulder. He let out a hiss before he charged and threw his weight into the monster. When he did, he placed his hand on the Rogue's chest, and in a matter of seconds, ice formed beneath his fingers, spreading rapidly until it covered the length of the body. The Rogue continued screaming until his last breath was sucked out by shards of ice in his throat. In a final gesture, Draven raised his silver blade and brought it crushing down upon the frozen body to shatter it into a million tiny pieces, skittering across the concrete floor by his feet.

The fight with the rabids inside was done. The group was destroyed. He didn't know how the fight fared outside with the other Guardians and the Fallens that had arrived to offer their services.

Turning again, he saw that in the moment,

Zarah was close to Nathanial's face. She was saying something, but he was too far away to hear. Then her power swelled, electrifying the air around the entire base. Nathanial began to scream, choking from her grip.

Thomas approached and stood by Draven as the two watched from a distance, cloaked in the shadows and the destruction of the slaughtered Rogues, as Zarah began to slowly destroy Nathanial. Despite the poison in her system, she didn't lunge for his neck to have his blood. He didn't have enough honor for that kind of easy death. Draven didn't blame her. He wouldn't have done it either.

He swallowed a forming lump in his throat.

Nathanial was burning from the inside out. Smoke curled in a slow dancing rhythm toward the ceiling, before the fire erupted along his pale skin, leaving a stench that burned Draven's senses. In seconds, ashes of their former mentor and boss fell softly through her slender fingers before floating through the air. It was apparent her "gift" was fire...but was it everything? Zarah stared down at her hands questioningly.

She turned and saw him then, the violet glow immediately fading and exhaustion taking over her features. He took a tentative step toward her when she started toward him. But when she began to collapse, he ran, catching her before she could hit the concrete.

****

"Draven," she whispered, realizing he had caught her.

"I'm here. You're okay. We got you." His voice came out in a rush, and he pushed her hair away from her face.

All of the power had drained her completely. The poison in her system was doing its work again. The only way to combat it would be to feed. Draven was hugging her and she could smell him. It made her lick her lips. That glorious scent—cherry and rich spices that were like no other—filled her and she had to suck in a deep breath to keep her hunger down.

Draven must have sensed it though. He pulled back and stared deeply into her eyes, tracing a finger over the thin cut on her cheek, before glancing back to where Thomas has been. She followed his eyes. Her brother was no longer there, probably having gone out to check on the fight there.

Quickly, he pulled her back against him and turned his head.

"Go ahead," he whispered. "You need it."

"You told me if I ever fed from you, you'd kick my ass," she tried to joke. Her voice came out weak and slow.

"We'll deal with that later," he replied, his voice carrying a smirk that she couldn't see. His fingers tenderly played through strands of her hair. She smiled at his touch.

"Wow, if I'm getting this lucky, maybe I can

get you to cross-stitch with me sometime, too." He tensed and quickly shook his head.

"No, that's all yours."

She softly laughed, but it ended on a cough. He pushed her into the crook of his neck further to entice her.

Zarah leaned into him. His scent grew heavier as she neared the hollow of his throat, and beneath her hand on his chest, his heart beat rapidly. It was a funny thing to feel it, knowing that they were a supposed risen-from-the-dead race of creatures. Yet they still had beating hearts and emotions. Perhaps even a soul. A human female and vampire male could bear children.

She closed her eyes and listened to his pulse for a few beats before her teeth finally sank into the soft flesh.

Draven emitted an automatic low growl and gripped her tighter against him as she fed. She savored the glorious flavors that danced over her taste buds, already beginning to return her strength. The rush of his cold blood tasted rich and electrifying. Her eyes sprang open, and her hand tenderly found a grip in his hair. Only seconds passed before she pulled away again, not wanting to overtake his offering, and the exhaustion continued to wear her thin. Still, it was enough to start healing the poison in her body.

She pulled back and looked into his eyes again. That's when she noted the change. The silver and violet flecks that sparkled within his irises shone back down at her and she groaned.

"I'm sorry," she whispered, turning her head in shame.

"For what?" Draven sounded confused.

"Everything, but mostly, the change that's occurred within you. Because of me, you're different. A new species so I've been told."

He turned her face gently back toward him. "I'm not sorry. We'll get through this okay?"

Slowly, she nodded and sighed. Her eyes were drooping. She heard sirens and the helicopter again.

"Am I hearing things?" she asked quietly,

confused, focusing on the sounds.

"No. Those are humans. They're close. We need to get out of here soon."

"It's too late, Draven. I have a feeling they already know."

With that, she closed her eyes and breathed deep. He knew she was likely right and uneasiness creased his eyes. Standing, he cradled her in his arms and began to trek back across the bay to meet the others. Except when he turned, he saw them standing at the large rollaway doors already waiting on him. The massive forms of the Fallens took up a lot of the space. Seth was frowning, holding a large golden sword, as he looked around the bay at the destruction. And then his eyes landed on Zarah.

She could sense them, causing her eyes to open again.

"Are those—" she started in awe.

"Yes. They're Fallens. They came to help as a favor to fulfill from your mother's last request."

Zarah almost dropped from his arms from the shock at the mention of her mother, but didn't say anything else. Instead she just held her arms around his neck as he continued to carry her toward the group, resting her head against his shoulder, and stared at the Fallen in the front with curiosity.

"Everything in order?" Draven directed toward the group at no one in particular as he approached closer.

"Not quite," Thomas replied.

"Humans are at the fence line. Police, military, media. 'Copter is circling around, and it's a news reporter. So everything has been caught on camera. We can get out of here through the back, but our species is definitely public now. It'll be world news within forty-eight hours."

Zarah heard and while she was concerned, she was also busy staring at the Fallen. She didn't know much about their kind other than some never-ending war between them and Vampires. They did not seek each other out on the streets for battle though; most lived in secret as humans. Seeing them there to help on behalf of her mother filled her with curiosity, and her eyes wandered tiredly over each of them.

Then the one in front gazed down at her after looking over the destruction behind them, his face stern and his gold eyes stormy.

"She should be destroyed," he rumbled.

Twenty-Eight

"What?" Draven and Thomas both shouted, facing the Fallen. Zarah hunkered down more into Draven's arms as he pulled in more tightly, protective, and her brother stepped in front of them.

The band of Fallens stepped forward, still holding their strange swords. They were large, their wings intimidating. Zarah saw the other Guardians, the surviving ones from the Compound, quickly step beside them, holding their weapons as well.

"I don't understand, Seth," Thomas finally spoke through gritted teeth. Zarah realized he was addressing the leader.

"I thought you were on our side."

The Fallen rolled his eyes and sheathed his sword. Zarah noted his eyes were brighter, a brilliant gold that shone against his ivory skin. His long strawberry-blonde hair brushed his bare shoulders in waves. All of them had gold eyes, but their own differences. Unique hair colors, skin tones, body builds. But they were all bare-chested and wore black, baggy military style pants with boots.

"I'm not on your side. We are never on your side," Seth said with a dark laugh, causing her thoughts to be interrupted as she turned her attention back. She eyed the scene nervously, wondering if this was how she was going to really die. Surely they wouldn't be able to defeat a band of Fallen warriors.

They were running out of time standing around. Either they had to leave before the humans started storming the abandoned base, or before the sun started rising, which would be soon for both situations. Tired of waiting around, Zarah shifted her position so she could get a better view of Seth.

"Why are Fallens and Vamps at constant war anyway?" she blurted. She felt Draven's arms tense around her, and his fear that they were about to be in another battle—one they were sure to lose.

Seth gazed down at her with narrowed eyes, his look sending shivers down her spine.

"You'll find out one day."

"So, are you going to kill me or not?"

Everyone held their breath when she asked the question, not wavering as she continued staring up at him.

He stepped forward. Thomas and Draven started to stop him, but his warning glare faltered their steps.

"No, I'm not."

Then he reached forward and placed a large warm hand on her cheek where the cut was still trying to heal. Her body was still fighting some of the silver poisoning, despite having fed from Draven, because she didn't take enough and the use of her power had drained her. Warmth spread through her cheek and down her neck into her chest. She almost gasped. It wasn't uncomfortable; it felt beautiful and tender. He took his hand away too fast for her liking and she almost tried to grab it back. Draven frowned slightly at the reaction, but dismissed it when he saw Seth's hand pull away.

"You healed her?" He looked incredulous.

She looked at the Fallen, who was still staring down at her, and instinctively reached up to touch her face. The cut was gone, and she could feel the silver also healed completely from her system. So, why was she still so tired?

As if reading her mind, Seth nodded. "Yes, the poison is erased. But exhaustion is still prevalent because of the extensive use of power she used."

"Why?" she asked through tired eyes. "Why help me if you think I should be destroyed?"

He shrugged and looked around the base again.

"I guess you can say our band of warriors are rebels. Your world's version of Rogues perhaps? Your mother was one as well. Not the type that you obviously eradicate, of course. But we go against our Masters. You are granted to live from us, but you won't be so lucky should you meet any Fallen Warriors that follow the Masters. They will destroy you and any that follow you."

"I want to know more about this. About my mother, too," she whispered sleepily, yawning.

"You will in time, I'm sure. For now, we should go," he instructed, looking at the others. Everyone nodded in agreement and began making for the back exit as they heard human shouts coming from outside drawing closer toward the buildings.

"Thomas," Zarah said softly, reaching across and touching her brother's arm on their way out.

He looked over at her questioningly.

"Maybe I won't kill you after all."
She smirked at his stunned expression before falling asleep seconds later.

****

Warmth and light flooded her. Zarah stepped into a clean, empty room with pristine white walls and matching ceramic tile. Her body moved slowly as she looked around.

"Am I dreaming?" she asked out loud. Her voice came out echoed, and sounded soft and musical.

"Somewhat," a female voice responded behind her suddenly, causing her to turn and face her visitor.

Zarah gasped.
"Mom?"

"Hi, sweetheart," Kathleen said with a radiant smile, standing before Zarah and looking just as beautiful as she had before she'd died.

Zarah sucked in a sharp breath, afraid to touch her. Instead, her mother took the remaining steps toward her and pulled her into a tight embrace. Zarah's arms stayed limp at her sides, still in shock.

"Listen to me carefully. I don't have much time with you," Kathleen started in a rush after pulling back, keeping her hands steady on her shoulders.

"The world is about to change dramatically, and you are going to be a force to be reckoned with. You must learn to control and use your powers. You are so strong, baby girl. And start a change for as many as you can. The Fallen Masters already know and they'll be coming for you, so you're going to be up against more than just humans and rabids. I don't want to see you destroyed by the hands of the Masters the way I was."

"But I thought the Rogues—" Zarah started, confused.

Her mother smiled sadly and shook her head.

"No. I was an Exiled One. Once the Masters found my whereabouts, they ordered my destruction. I made sure not to let on that I had children or they would have destroyed you both as well."

"This is all so confusing. I have a lot of questions."

"I know. You will learn more in due time."

Zarah nodded slowly, knowing that her visit was coming to an end as tears sprang to her eyes.

"You've grown quite beautifully, sweetheart. Just as I always knew you would." Kathleen took a loose strand of Zarah's hair and tucked it back behind her ear. When her mother nodded and smiled, her short bobbed hair bounced with her, and her turquoise-gold eyes sparkled like glitter.

"It's time for you to wake up. Draven awaits, I'm sure. By the way, you should tell him to start looking more into his own past and family history. Just a thought."

When Zarah started to speak, Kathleen held up a hand to interrupt.

"Don't ask why, it's a suggestion that I think you should follow for the sake of the future."

She nodded and wiped away a few tears. "Will I ever see you again, Mom? Like this?"

"Not likely," Kathleen started, smiling sadly again and then reaching forward to place a hand on Zarah's chest.

"But know that I'm always in your heart, darling."

Her mother started to turn and walk away from her.

"Take care of your brother, too," she added before her form faded from sight and Zarah was left with a heavy emptiness.

****

There was a soft tickle on her cheek, slowly drawing her awake. Her eyes fluttered open to see Draven staring down at her with worry. He pulled his hand away. His fingers brushing across her cheek having been what awakened her, and smiled in relief when she stared up at him in silence.

The emptiness from the dream of her mother still weighed her down and she continued to fight the tears back.

Noticing she was in a bed, with Draven sitting beside her, she looked around briefly to see a large room that was well furnished. An office with all the current updated technology she could have imagined set off to the side in a separate space through an open doorway. She laid in a large wrought-iron bed with four posts that stood tall and proud, winding up toward the ceiling in an elegant leafed pattern. The floor was a dark cherry hardwood. Across the room, sat a black leather couch with a glass table beside it. A large, thin television hung on the wall in front of the bed.

"Where are we?" Her voice cracked.

"At the new Compound building we're establishing. It's, uh, above ground this time. So that will explain why you won't see any windows during daylight hours."

She paused and looked around again, seeing what he meant. Just like he said, she couldn't visibly see any windows. Instead she saw large sliding metal shutters locked in the place where the windows were meant to be. They looked motorized, and when she glanced on the wall near the draping burgundy curtains, she saw the control panel system that probably controlled them.

She noticed a shopping bag on the table in the sitting area. When he caught her gaze on it, he grew flustered, picking it up and carrying it over to her.

"I know you lost all of your belongings, so I went to a store before sunrise and bought some things."

She stared at him blankly, blinking a few

times, before turning to the bag and peeking inside. A soft smile turned up the corners of her mouth when she saw the items: several cross-stitching patterns with their threads and needles, some art paper and pencils, and a beading kit for making jewelry. It wasn't everything, but enough, and he'd thought of her.

"Thank you."
He nodded and cast his eyes down.

His nearness made her nervous, self-conscious. It was a new feeling that she hadn't experienced before. She bit her lip trying to think of more to say. Her eyes drifted back to him and she sighed, beginning to sit up.

"We're sharing this building with the Fallens. You should know that," he spoke slowly. He watched her cautiously.

She froze and clenched her jaw.
"Why? I thought they were going to leave?"

Draven stood and crossed the room in long strides. Maybe the closeness had made him nervous, too. She didn't know. Or perhaps, he was just falling back into his usual cold, Guardian routine and things were going to go back to where they had stood between them before. After all, she had changed him into a strange new being. Even she hated herself for that.

Zarah watched him silently, waiting for his response, as he walked over to a dresser and poured a couple of drinks. His face was emotionless when he turned and brought one back to her, keeping one for himself.

"Apparently not. Seth and his brothers want to stay. There's a lot already happening," he replied after a moment while she drank. She hadn't realized how thirsty she'd been until he handed her the glass.

Suddenly, Zarah thought of Thomas and frowned. Opening her senses, she immediately knew he was somewhere in the building there as well.

Draven jumped in alarm when she'd stood abruptly, thrusting her empty cup at him.

"I have something to take care of long overdue. Give me your gun and show me right now where Thomas is."

Twenty-Nine

Draven was tripping over his feet, stumbling over the end of the area rug, before he caught Zarah's arm. She'd already found his gun and was loading it.

Her hair was a long, tangled mess. It was apparent that someone, or Draven, had changed her shirt at least. The other one had been stained with blood. She was now wearing an oversized plain black shirt. Her jeans had been torn at the knees during the fighting, but she didn't care. She tossed out the question of whether Draven changed her shirt or not, ignoring her current appearance, and went about loading the ammunition.

Ignoring Draven's fumbling, she headed for the door.

"What are you going to do?" He grabbed her

arm, stopping her, as she started out in the hallway.

"I'm going to find Thomas. I know he's here." She yanked her arm back.

"You can take me to his room, it'd be quicker. Either way, I'll find him."

Zarah kept walking. She saw the distress and confusion in his eyes. He kept protesting.

"Zarah, I thought you said back at the base that you might not kill him? And really…can't you get past this now? He helped through a lot, and he'll continue helping us, I know. Besides, I met Ethan. I saw what happened to him. Maybe you can cure Thomas."

She swallowed and clenched her jaw. The truth was she was going to do exactly that. It was a big decision on her part. Since she had returned from being Rogue, her oath always had been to kill Thomas when given the chance. The last couple of months changed her.

Zarah didn't tell Draven he had nothing to worry about. Instead, she kept walking briskly through the hall with the gun in her hand at her side waiting for her senses to pick up on her brother, determination set in her features.

"Just take me to my brother."

Draven sighed and led her on in silence. When they stopped in front of her brother's apartment door, he looked again at her with pleading eyes. She rolled hers in response before banging on the door.

"Sis, good to see you're awake. I was about to come check on you—" Thomas began, standing in the doorway, before Zarah interrupted him.
"Let's cut the chat, okay?" she snapped and then aimed the gun eye level.

Thomas took a small step back but kept his gaze steady on her, frowning.
"I thought you said you changed your mind, hmm?" A smirk began to turn up the corner of his mouth. Draven fidgeted beside her uneasily. She

saw Alyssa in the dark room, staring at the scene in disbelief, but unmoving. The tension charged the air.

"Well, I lied I guess."

Thomas stared in amused silence before shrugging. He stepped back as pushed her way into the apartment. The gun remained aimed and steady on him, her eyes never leaving his face as she walked forward.

"Close the door, Draven." Zarah didn't bother turning to look at him while she barked the order when they were inside. She could hear him moving slowly, wary of her actions. He followed her command and then took a stance off to the side in a corner.

"Are you ready, Thomas?" Her eyebrows rose and a small teasing smile on her face matched his.

"Or are you going to try and delay me?"

Her eyes flitted over to Alyssa. The Rogue woman was standing at the back of the room near a desk, eyes filled with tears, but she remained still. Zarah didn't worry about her coming into a fight. Alyssa knew this was between brother and sister to resolve only.

"I've always been ready, little sister. I told you that when the time came, I looked forward to dying by your hand."

Zarah's jaw clenched. Of course he was. She knew the truth. She'd learned enough from Nathanial. The ambush. His turning. It had all been a set-up because Thomas knew what she was all along. He knew turning her would trigger her gene, bringing her immunity and Fallen power out full-force. The more memories flooded her of the night he had turned her Rogue, the more she started understanding. Yes, he had been smiling that night when he'd closed her in the dark, and at that time it had seemed malicious, but then she recalled his eyes—cold, deep burgundy eyes that carried the weight of a heavy apology and intense sorrow. Zarah couldn't get the memory from her mind, and even with him standing before her then, his eyes still shone with the same sad intensity despite the playful smile on his face.

"Don't do this, Zarah," Draven's voice cut into her thoughts.
"Shut up, Draven."

"Yes, shut it, Guardian. This is between me and my sister. We knew this was going to happen," Thomas remarked, his eyes still steady on her.
"You have no idea," she started, stepping closer and closer until she touched the gun to his chest. If she really wanted to threaten him, she'd have held it to his temple, but she had other plans. He wasn't suspicious in the least.
"You have no idea how much hell I went through because of you."
Her voice was a low whisper and tears were beginning to sting at the corners of her eyes as she struggled for the words. No, she wouldn't forgive easily. But she would try, and she would save him. Besides, she needed him more than ever now.

"Zarah...I know. And I can't emphasize how sorry I am. Of course, that won't save me. I don't deserve to be, anyway. I want you to kill me. Do it. Quit stalling."

Suddenly she smiled, brilliantly bright. With a flash, she brought the gun down and fired, grazing her brother's foot. He screamed out a curse and leapt backwards with a limp.

"What the hell? I meant quickly! Not torture!" he yelled, reaching for his bleeding foot while he collapsed into a nearby chair.

"I'm not going to kill you, Thomas," Zarah said softly, setting the gun down on the table. Everyone in the room looked at her incredulously.

"So, you just shot me in the foot for sport?"

"Mostly."

Thomas growled and shook his head in disbelief.

"Actually," she started, "I shot you in the foot so you'd not only sit there with what I'm about to make you do, but so that you have some silver poisoning slowly beginning to form in your system and would need this either way."

He looked confused. But Draven had worked it out, already stepping toward Zarah in shock.

"You shouldn't have worried me like that," Draven hissed through his teeth, causing her to let out a soft laugh.

"I'm serious, Zarah, I thought you were really going to kill him."

She spun around to face him and narrowed her eyes.

"I thought so, too."

Dropping the subject, she turned back to her confused brother who was still nursing his injured foot. Alyssa had finally built the courage to approach and stood beside her mate with concern.

Zarah took a fingernail and sliced a thin line across her wrist before thrusting it at Thomas.

"You're going to feed from me. That's why

I'm here. That's why I'm not killing you."

Her brother stared at her in disbelief. She gave him an encouraging smile and pushed her wrist closer.

"If you do this, it'll not only cure you, but then you can cure Alyssa. Yeah, we're going to be a new race, but something tells me that it's important, Thomas." Zarah kept the bit about the dream of their mother to herself for the time being.

After a brief hesitation, he nodded, swallowing nervously.

"I just don't want to hurt you...again."

"You won't."

She watched him spare Alyssa a glance for reassurance. When she nodded, reaching out and taking his hand in hers, he turned back to Zarah and sighed. Bringing Alyssa's life into it as well had helped make his mind up. Knowing Thomas could save her too was enough for him to make the decision.

"Alright."

Zarah saw Draven step up beside her protectively as Thomas began drinking from her wrist. She knew it was taking a lot of his strength to fight his Rogue instincts from caving to the bloodlust. She remembered that dark menacing voice that once resided at the back of her own mind, enticing her to gorge until all of the blood was drained. But she knew he was a fighter. He always had been. His Fallen gene wasn't the only thing that helped him maintain a level of control even for a Rogue; it was his own strength, too.

After a few minutes, Thomas pulled away with a gasp. The changes were already starting as she saw the exhaustion taking over when she pulled away. He swayed in the chair and clutched at his temple like Ethan had done. The small change wouldn't take long.

"We'll let you rest. I'll see you later," Zarah said, directing Draven to follow her out.

"Stay with us as long as you like. Just don't annoy the hell out of me."

Thomas snorted a pained chuckle.

"Yeah, right. You know I always like to annoy you, Sis."

She smirked and continued out the door with Draven.

Thirty

"I'm glad you forgave him—" Draven started after they left the room. Relief flooded his voice and reached the growing smile on his face.

Zarah stopped and spun around so quickly that he nearly ran into her.

"I didn't forgive him. It'll be a long time for that process to go through. I merely just decided not to kill him."

"Why then?"

"Why then, what?" she asked, crossing her arms over her chest with a frown.

"Why did you decide not to kill him?" His smile had disappeared, replaced with an unreadable expression and stern eyes.

She swallowed and dropped her gaze. Sighing, she shrugged.

"Because he's my brother and the only family I have left. It was only right, especially since I had a way to save him. It's what my mother would have wanted also, I think." Zarah's reply was soft as she shuffled her bare feet back and forth on the cold hallway tiles. The new building did not have the blindingly white hallways like the underground base had. These were a more muted ivory with a blue pattern, and had a classic, yet high-cost feel.

Then after a pause, "He probably would have done the same for me if the roles had been reversed."

"Exactly."

"Hey, have you two been watching the news?" Seth's voice suddenly cut through the hall, coming toward them.

Zarah turned to see the Fallen looking extremely...human. He was even wearing plaid pajama pants and a white tee. She must've let her confusion show because he smirked at her.

"Our wings don't have a constant appearance, Zarah," he said as if reading her thoughts.

Quickly shaking her head to dislodge the distraction, she laughed nervously. Of course she knew that.

"Right. I should have known. Anyways, what's this about the news?"

"Oh, yeah, have you both been watching?" he asked again.

They both shook their heads.
"No, we had an issue to handle," she explained.

Seth nodded slowly and then motioned for them to follow.

"I think you need to see."

****

When they walked into the Lounge, Zarah was surprised to see most of everyone there. She recognized Guardians that had survived the earlier attack. Jerry, Nicholas, James, Markus, and Braydon. The Fallens were there, all eight of them, including Seth, she counted. She needed to learn the others' names still. Either way, she suddenly noticed she was the only female in the room. In all, her and Alyssa were going to be outnumbered by the testosterone. The thought didn't affect her much. She was used to it, having been one of the only female Guardians before as well.

The room had been buzzing with conversation when they'd entered. A large screen television was switched on in the corner of the room while everyone lounged on couches and chairs. But then the silence stretched when they looked up and saw Zarah standing in the doorway.

She ignored their stares and instead focused on the news. There was an image coming across the screen, constantly being repeated. The United States Capital was facing a lot of panicked humans. There were protestors waving signs pleading the President to "flush-out" the vamps before they take over, people attacking others if they looked like a vampire. Which, of course, was often wrong because the people getting attacked were only defenseless humans that liked the darker fashions.

In twenty-four hours, everything had already become an uproar.

She could feel both Draven and Seth watching her intently. It made her uncomfortable to be under their gaze.

"We can't allow Vampires to live in this world! Haven't you read anything in the last hundred and fifty years? They'll enslave us!" One citizen shouted into a reporter's microphone.

"Is this news only spread in America?" She started to suggest packing it up and leaving the country, but frowned knowing how ridiculous it sounded. Even if it wasn't world-wide yet, it would be a matter of a few more hours before it was.

"It's already breaking international news organizations," Seth replied, changing the channel on the television. Then she saw women crying in a panic, and men screaming curses in Spanish when she realized that Seth had put it on a foreign station. They were showing images of citizens in Spain. Zarah shook her head in disbelief.

"What about you guys? Were you seen?" She was frowning at Seth, then directed her glare around the room at the group of Fallen residing with them. He shook his head with a sly smile.

"I guess we were lucky." She heard the mocking tone in his deep voice. There was an unusual accent there she hadn't heard before.

"Yeah, I guess so." Her arms crossed over chest in annoyance.

"Zarah," Jerry cut in, standing from his seat and stepping forward. She turned and looked at the Guardian to see his eyes were full of determination and admiration. Suddenly, the others were standing, too. In any other situation, she would have felt nervous, but when she looked around at the Guardians, all she saw were pride and respect.

"We heard you can create a new race of Vampires—ones with a special power like you and Draven," Jerry continued. She stared silently at him, waiting for the sneers or the disgust, but it never came.

"Yes."

"Change us."

She looked at them in shock. "Do you even know what you're asking?"

"We know exactly what we're asking. We're asking for you to change us. Make us a part of a new race. The world is about to drastically change. There's most likely going to be some very dark times ahead. War. Let's start building our own army. We want you to lead us."

She sucked in a deep breath and looked around at the guys. Catching Seth's gaze, she was slightly relieved to see the Fallen not seeming affected by the Guardians so open by her changing them. She remembered their reaction to her when they first picked her up at the base. Turning to Draven, he nodded his encouragement but remained silent.

"Alright," she finally said.

Her eyes strayed back to the television and there she saw the aerial video clips of their fighting at the base, occasionally being zoomed in on a Rogue whenever one hissed and bared its elongated fangs. Those were the images the humans were being shown. They were spared from the truth—they wouldn't know the amount of countless hours spent that Guardians and other Vampires had always protected humans. She could still remember her years of training before being brought onto the team and how important it was to always maintain the attitude that humans should be helped, not harmed. They could work in peace together secretly but with the impending future, Zarah knew it was no longer going to be possible. There were going to be too many stereotypes and too many Vampires who wanted the opportunity for superiority.

"For now, let's just party like it's the end of the world," a voice came from the doorway.

Everyone turned to see Thomas and Alyssa standing there. Zarah noticed the amused smirk on his face before she saw his eyes. The old, red rabid color was gone, replaced with a mix of amber and gold. Her brother was back. She almost laughed out loud when seeing the others' stunned expressions. Draven did laugh beside her causing warmth to blossom in her chest.

"I do believe it may already be the end of the world, Thomas," Zarah said sarcastically, returning his smirk.

Epilogue

As Thomas had announced, there'd been a party. Perhaps not really much of one, but they all let loose for a while at least trying to forget the current worries. They waited until the next night to gather up again so everyone could catch up on rest, and Zarah could get a shower and a change of clothes.

The news was switched off. Instead, someone turned on a stereo and began blasting music—some of Zarah's favorite heavy rock bands—as everyone began taking turns playing each other against various games of pool or foosball. A couple of the guys pulled out a game console. The noise and laughter that echoed around the room made her smile when she entered.

No one talked about the issues they were going to have to worry about soon. They were talking about anything and everything else. The windows opened as night rose and she enjoyed the view over the city. Apparently the new Compound was its own building, seven stories high, where most of their activity and living quarters were on the top floor.

Draven was distant from her again. In a way, it bothered her. Hurt. Over the past couple of months, she knew she had developed feelings for him. She would have to clamp them down so she could focus on the coming work ahead of them.

She had to take a break from the crowd so she stepped onto the adjoining balcony from the Lounge. The wind outside was cold, but the chill didn't affect her. Zarah ran her hands along the balcony railing, looking down at the passing humans on the street.

"You look like your mother. I don't think I've managed to say that to you yet." Seth's voice carried to her from the doorway.

Zarah turned and saw him stepping up beside her, looking out over the city and not at her. His face showed no signs of emotions. His strawberry-blonde hair ruffled lightly against the night breeze and she surprisingly picked up a scent. Seth smelled like vanilla.

"Thank you." Her words came out quiet, a bit unnerved from his comment. He nodded and then turned his heavy gaze, his eyes darker amber than before, on her as if he waited for her to continue. She swallowed nervously.

"How did you know her, anyway?"

"She was an Exiled One. She saved me once."

She nodded as if she understood but didn't ask him to elaborate the story. Maybe he would tell her more one day. He didn't seem much up to telling her more than that then.

Zarah turned away from the city view and looked back into the Lounge at everyone. She stared at Draven for a long time in silence. Her mother had told her to start looking into Draven's past. Was that a good or bad thing? What would she find if she started digging around? And should she go to him about it at all? Questions seemed to nag at her a lot recently that she was struggling to find answers to.

"I talked to her in a dream. My mother. Does that sound crazy?" she asked Seth.

"No. She is still a part of the spirit world. Kathleen needed to reach you, so I believe that she would have found a way."

Zarah felt a weight lifted from her as she took a deep breath and nodded.

"So, Seth, can I trust you?"
Her fingers thrummed the railing nervously.

He blinked at her sudden mood and subject change. Then, a slow, mischievous smile spread across his gorgeous face.

"I'm still a Fallen. It's wise that you never trust one of us." With that, he leaned forward and placed a kiss on her cheek before leaving her alone on the balcony. His lips were soft and left tingling, warm stirring waves flowing over her skin. She stared after him in shock, her mouth agape. Surely he had seen the way she stared at Draven, sensed the way she felt? Why would he do that?

When her eyes darted to Draven, she knew he had seen what happened by the way he glared darkly across the room at her before leaving.

She had no time to protest, to go explain anything to him, because then shots started echoing through the streets of the city and sirens blared. She glanced around.

"Well, it seems war has started a bit quicker than expected."

Acknowledgments

All I've known since childhood was that I wanted to write. Even before I could lift a pen, I was telling stories and creating characters. My imagination has always been a bit chaotic, but without it, I wouldn't have met the amazing beings that bounce around in my head on a daily basis.

Of course, I've had many people along the way to thank for the support while I chase after my crazy dreams. Thank you to all of my great family. I'd name you all, but I don't have the space. You know I love you though! Steven, I stay up so many late nights "cheating" with my characters. I'm glad you've got used to that. Jerry, you're a rocking brother. Of course, your name is in here. Thanks to you and Kim for the support, in both writing and life.

To my best friend, Chasity Grigsby, who has been a huge part of my life for almost twenty years.

I'd also like to acknowledge Kelly Watt, a great friend and confidant, and writing partner. Through a lot of critique and commentary, we have helped each other out through the years. Thank you, Kelly.

To Kara Malinczak for partial editing help and commentary. Without her, I would still be on my first draft. A big thank you goes out to my friend and wonderfully talented, Taylor Jenkins. My book cover would not have been possible without her crafty skills. She also has been a great writing partner and book chat buddy through the years.

Last but not least, as a book blogger myself, I have to make a very large acknowledgement to the book blogging community. Without this amazing online community, authors like myself would not be here. I have made some amazing friends through the community (Lea, Kara, Shanella, Kristin—I wish I could name you all, too!). Every one of you are wonderful and I wish I could give you a great big hug and dozens of chocolate chip cookies.

About the Author

Pixie Lynn Whitfield resides in Texas with her husband and three kids. She is constantly writing or has her nose in a book. When she's not writing or reading, she has a mild obsession with baseball and music. You can find her online through Twitter, Goodreads, or her book blog at http://the-bookaholic.blogspot.com. The second book to *The Guardians of the Night* trilogy is due out in early 2013.